THE DEVIL'S ADVOCATE

HELL'S ANGEL BOOK TWO

JANE HINCHEY

AUTHOR'S NOTE

Dear Reader,

Big news in my literary world! As you know, I've been writing as both Jane Hinchey and Zahra Stone. It's been quite the adventure, but now it's time for a change. I'm bringing everything back under my original name, Jane Hinchey. Just like my stories, life has its twists, and this is the latest one for me.

What does this mean for your Zahra Stone favorites? They're getting a fresh look with my real name, but the stories inside are the same ones you love.

As you delve into The Devil's Advocate, you're not just reading a story, but joining me on my author's journey. Your support has been invaluable, and I'm so grateful for it.

Here's to more mystery, more romance, and more adventures together!

xoxo

Jane

The world needs a hero. Might as well be me.

Seeing as I'm the devil, you'd think that I'd be ecstatic to find out that Heaven is dying.

Well, I'm not... Because with those pearly gates closed, all new souls either end up in my domain or completely lost with nowhere to go.

God is missing, and so is my boyfriend.

To save both, I'll need to unleash the apocalypse. Of course, my nosy, good-for-nothing Archangel brothers won't make that easy.

Yeah, I'm just your average, everyday fallen angel, but I'm also the world's last hope. Can I find God, rebuild Heaven, and save the earth from certain destruction, all while keeping the flame alive with my fire demon boyfriend? Let's find out, shall we?

"What do you mean, the sword is gone?"

I spun, pinning Dacian with a glare. My fury at losing Levi had settled into cold, hard determination. Already, I was planning to get Levi back using the glowing sword my brother Gabriel had turned against me. Clearly, a weapon forged in Heaven that could do me harm.

A powerful weapon. One that could be used to force our way into another realm.

Crossing his arms over his chest, Dacian returned my glare, unconcerned with being on the receiving end of my burning gaze. "I threw it to Levi as the portal closed."

"So he has it?"

"I saw him catch it," Dacian confirmed.

Well, that was good. Levi had a weapon and a way to get back through the portal— assuming the sword worked for him. He was a human, after all. At the very least, he could use it to protect himself from Zuska, the soul stealer who'd dragged him through the portal into another dimension.

"Wait!" It suddenly hit me. "How did you have the sword? Last I saw, Gabriel had it."

We'd been in the caverns beneath Shadow Falls. The giant orb Gabriel had hidden there was powerful enough to wipe the humans from the planet. When we'd combined our powers to stop the orb, the whole thing had exploded, and we'd somehow been transported to the cemetery, to the portal. Gabriel had not.

"I called for it." Dacian shrugged as if I'd know what that meant.

"I don't have time for this bullshit, Dacian." My patience was thin, my thoughts consumed by Levi. I prayed he'd survived the journey through the portal. Goodness only knows what awaited him on the other side.

Dacian blew out a breath and ran a hand through his hair. "Okay, fine. The sword is called the Sword of Angels. It's Heaven's ultimate weapon."

"And my brothers have it," I muttered. It figured. Two idiots wielding a powerful weapon and all too happy to use it against their sister.

"They *had* it," Dacian corrected me. "Now Levi has it."

"But he's human. Will it work for him?"

"Possibly."

"Possibly isn't good enough, Dacian!" My yell made him jump, and he frowned at me. "Tell me everything you know about the Sword of Angels—or whatever you called it—everything!"

"I only know what it told me," he began. "The first time I saw it was when the ghosts used it against you. Apparently, Gabriel was the one who gave them the sword. He wanted to banish you from Earth and send you back to Hell."

I wasn't surprised. I'd guessed one of my brothers was behind the zombie ghost attack.

"Only he never thought the sword would end up in my possession. Once it was...it was like a connection. I knew where it came from. I understood its powers. It was like a psychic link."

"Is it because you're a Seraph Angel?" I asked. "A protector?"

"I think so. When I saw Levi being pulled through the portal, I thought, 'If only the sword were here'…and then it appeared in my hand. It was reflex to throw it to Levi."

"I'm glad you did. Thank you."

I turned away, pacing in front of the headstones. We no longer had the Sword of Angels at our disposal. I couldn't open the portal with my magic; I'd tried and failed. We needed brute force. And I could think of only one place where such power existed.

"We need to go to Heaven," I decided. "My brothers are responsible for this, and if we combine our powers, we should be able to get the portal open. Long enough for me to retrieve Levi, at any rate."

"You think they will help you?" The surprise in Dacian's voice was unmistakable.

"If they want the Sword of Angels back, they will."

It had been a few millennia since I last stood in front of the Pearly Gates, and to say I was shocked was an understatement.

"What's going on?" For as far as the eye could see, there were souls, all milling around waiting for the gates to open. "The gates are locked? Why?"

"They have been closed for some time." Dacian's voice was grim as he studied the bedraggled souls huddled on the steps.

"But all these souls...displaced." I couldn't hide my shock. Why would my father not allow them into Heaven? If they had sins to atone for, they would have been redirected to Hell, so they were in the right place, Heaven-bound.

"Heaven isn't what you remember, Lucy. What Gabriel said about Heaven dying? It's true. There's a sickness pervading our realm, and I suspect the gates are locked because Heaven no longer has the capacity to house new souls."

"Why didn't you tell me this before?"

Dacian shrugged. "It's not your concern. Hell is your jurisdiction, not Heaven."

I felt the sting of irritation dance over my skin. Grabbing his arm, I forced him to look at me. "This *was* my home. My father is here, my brothers...my *family*. Of course it's my concern. You should have told me."

"Perhaps. It was not my call to make. I'm just a Seraph Angel. I don't make the decisions."

"Fine. Let's talk to the person who does. Can you

get us past the gates?" While we'd been talking, I'd touched the gates, tried to open them, but they wouldn't budge for me.

"I can. Take my hand."

He held his palm out to me, and I slipped my hand into his. A memory from eons ago flashed into my mind of the first time Dacian held my hand and the silly little skip of delight I'd felt. How things had changed.

In more ways than one, it seemed. Inside the gates, I glanced around, and my breath caught in my throat. Heaven looked...dirty. The once white buildings were now a dull grey. Some of them were crumbling, and debris littered the streets. Broken-down vehicles had been left, abandoned, on the roads.

"Remind you of anything?" Dacian spoke softly behind me.

I nodded. "Yes. This is just like before Hell was created before the evil souls were banished."

"Exactly."

"You think that's what's causing this? Has evil retaken hold of Heaven?"

I was puzzled how that could be. Initially, when God created Heaven and Earth, he hadn't accounted for the fallout of the free will he'd gifted to humans.

When their mortal time was up on Earth, and their souls arrived in Heaven, the evil ones had tainted Heaven. As a consequence, God had created Hell and given me responsibility for it, an honor I gladly accepted.

"It could be that, or..." Dacian trailed off, shifting his weight from foot to foot.

"What?" I knew he was avoiding telling me, which meant it was bad.

"Maybe Heaven is like this because God is sick."

I absorbed his words. God was immortal; we all were. But we had weaknesses. There had to be a balance, and as much as it pained me to admit it, maybe Dacian was right. That would explain why my brothers were getting away with such outrageous behavior. There was only one way to know for sure.

Find Dad and see for myself exactly what was going on.

Heaven Central was as busy as ever as we pulled up in our sleek, silver vehicle. Thankfully, the transportation system was still functioning, and driverless vehicles zipped around the streets, catering to the humans who had ascended after their time on Earth was over. They didn't have wings, so they needed transportation.

"I'm getting a really weird feeling of deja-vu," I muttered, stepping out of the vehicle with Dacian close behind me.

"Same."

It was eerily similar to that time, thousands of years ago when we'd come to the Angel Towers building on Golden Wing Avenue to confront my brothers about the deteriorating state of Heaven. And even though we'd managed to rectify the situation then, I had a funny feeling in the pit of my stomach that things were going to be very different this time.

As I strode across the foyer, I changed my outfit from the designer jeans I'd worn on Earth to a black, figure-hugging Prada dress and red Louis Vuitton heels. My hair twisted itself up into a French braid at the back of my head, and my favorite gold bracelet appeared on my wrist.

"Power dressing?" Dacian inquired.

"You bet."

The elevator opened as we approached. We stepped inside and rode it up.

Dacian broke the silence. "Who do we see first?"

I glanced at him out of the corner of my eye. "Dad. I need to check that he's okay, that this latest problem with Heaven isn't to do with his health. And I had a thought—he can retrieve Levi from the Xoelax dimension. I don't need Michael or Gabriel for that." A little bit of research had revealed that the soul stealer who'd taken Levi was from Xoelax, a fact I wished I'd known before now. I'm not sure how it would have helped, but I hated not having all the facts.

"Good point, but will he interfere? He never has before now."

"I think he can be persuaded. After all, it was Gabriel who was negotiating with the Xoelax people to bring the orb to Earth in the first place. As Vice President of Invention, he's supposed to make sure no alien technology ever makes its way to earth. This is a direct conflict. The least Dad can do is retrieve one human and then see that Gabriel is reprimanded."

"That's a reach," Dacian muttered, moving in behind me as the elevator stopped and the doors opened onto the boardroom of Angel Towers.

"Lucifer." Gabriel stood, pushing back his chair from the head of the table. Why was he sitting in Dad's seat? To his left lounged Michael, who didn't greet me at all, just stared. Nothing had changed, I saw.

"I take it you were alerted to my arrival." Striding over to the opposite end of the table, I placed my palms against it and leaned forward. "Where's Dad? I need to talk to him."

Gabriel and Michael exchanged a look. "He's... indisposed right now. You'll have to make do with us."

"Not going to happen. I'm not leaving here until

I see him." I pulled out a chair and sank into its plush depths, crossing my legs and idly studying my fingernails. I was prepared to wait them out. I could be as stubborn as them when I wanted to be.

"Dacian, report to HR. You disobeyed us, and there are consequences," Michael ordered, continuing to ignore me.

As Dacian spun to obey, I stopped him with a hand on his wrist. "Don't go to HR. Wait for me downstairs."

I kept my voice low, trying to convey to Dacian without words why I didn't want him reporting to HR. I was pretty sure my brothers had employed some sort of mind-altering program on Dacian, and it was entirely possible they conducted it via HR. Dacian inclined his head slightly and left.

Michael finally turned his attention to me. "He isn't here."

"Who?"

"God. Father. Dad. He isn't here."

"What do you mean, he isn't here? As in, at Angel Towers?"

"No, as in, not in Heaven."

"Where is he, then?" If he wasn't in Heaven, and he wasn't in Hell, where exactly was he? Visiting Earth?

"We don't know. He's missing." Michael's voice was cold and flat, devoid of any trace of emotion. I, however, had enough emotion for both of us. Anxiety, anger, worry—they all danced through me, raising goosebumps on my arms and making my stomach churn. This was bad. And what they were about to tell me next was really bad. I could feel it. I wanted to puke but swallowed and did my best to hide my reaction from my brothers.

"How long has he been missing?" I applauded myself for keeping my voice so calm when all I wanted to do was scream and shout and rant at them.

"Since you left," Gabriel said.

I shifted my attention to him. He, too, was cold and calm. It was all starting to make sense in a horrific and sick way. How Earth was falling apart. How the humans were not only destroying themselves but the planet along with them. I'd often wondered why Dad never intervened, but now I understood—because he wasn't here. He was missing. He'd been missing since Hell was created. And that was a long time ago.

"Is that why Heaven is dying? Because Dad..." I had to stop and clear my throat. "Because Dad is?"

Gabriel shrugged, exchanging a look with Michael.

"How could you!" I exploded. I was so angry there must have been fire in my eyes. "How could you keep this from me? I'm his daughter. You aren't the only ones this affects!"

"See? I told you she'd have hysterics," Michael said to Gabriel.

I couldn't contain myself. I darted around the table and pressed a flaming wing to his throat. He shrank back in his chair, horrified, as I let the fire dance across his skin. It wasn't enough to burn, but I could change that with a mere thought—and oh, how I dearly wanted to let my flames burn until he was consumed by them.

"Lucy, settle down." Gabriel didn't sound concerned, merely bored, as he watched. "This is precisely why we didn't tell you. You tend to overreact." I could taste the untruth in the air. It was thick, heavy, and dark. I almost choked on it.

"Since when do we lie in Heaven?" I put my wings away and arched a brow at Gabriel, my voice deadly calm. Gabriel shrugged. "This is why everything has turned to shit on Earth, isn't it? Droughts, famine, war, violence. You've let it all go unpoliced, totally unconcerned. Why?"

I caught that look again between Gabriel and Michael, and I was fed up with it. Sick of their bullshit and plotting and planning.

"Same reason you planted that orb from Xoelax, isn't it?" I guessed. "You want Earth for yourselves, and with dad out of the way...you figure you'll let the humans destroy themselves."

"She is smart. I'll give her that," Gabriel drawled.

I pinned him with my gaze. "But you were too impatient, Gabriel. You wanted to hurry things along, bring in the orb to wipe out the humans. And that was your mistake because with the soul stealer running amok on Earth, that got *my* attention. And here we are. You're busted." I crossed my arms over my chest. *Wriggle out of this one, asshole.*

"And tell me, Lucy, just what are you going to do about it? Dear old Dad doesn't give a crap about any of us, clearly."

Damn it, he had a point. What was I going to do about it?

"Find him, of course."

Michael scoffed. "You don't think we haven't tried?"

"Oh, I'm sure you gave it a half-hearted effort, but no, I don't think you seriously looked. I don't think you put all your resources into it. You're the

Vice President of Defense, Michael. You could have an army out looking for him. Do you?"

The silence spoke volumes. It was as I suspected. My brothers didn't want our father found. Were they responsible for his disappearance in the first place? Surely not.

Surely they wouldn't stoop that low.

"Why did you want to see him, anyway?" Gabriel asked.

"I need his help to retrieve a human from a pocket dimension."

"Ah, would that be the same human who was helping you on Earth? The psychic?"

"What do you know of Levi?" My brows pulled together so tight they hurt. Had this been another of Gabriel's plans, to take Levi from me because I loved him?

"I can sense your anguish, sister dear. It doesn't take a genius to figure it out."

Michael barked out a laugh at Gabriel's taunt, and I sat back in my chair, regrouping.

"I suppose you want our help since Dad isn't here?" Gabriel asked.

I didn't move, waiting for him to drop his trump card. Gabriel had forgotten that while he was able to read me like a book, I could do the same to him. He was as predictable as he thought I was.

"No can do, sorry," Michael joined in. "We're busy here. Looking for God."

"So you don't need the Sword of Angels back, then?" I asked, studying my fingernails.

"What?" they said in unison.

I couldn't contain the grin splitting my face. "Levi had the Sword of Angels when he was dragged into the pocket dimension. It's stuck there with him. Since you aren't prepared to help me, I can only assume the sword isn't important to you anymore?"

I watched the furious exchange of facial expressions between my brothers, knew they were communicating telepathically. I did my best to appear calm and patient when in reality, I was ready to bombard them both with a barrage of fireballs. *Deep breaths, Lucy, deep breaths. You've got to play this right.*

"We can't leave Heaven. Not at this time," Gabriel said, with Michael nodding beside him.

"So you won't help?"

"That's not what I said." He glowered, a new look for Gabriel, and I bit back a smile at the constipated expression on his face.

"Oh?"

"You can retrieve your human pet yourself. You don't need our help."

"How? I tried to open the portal, but my magic isn't strong enough. I'm not waiting until All Hallows' Eve again." That was still a year away, and there was no way I'd leave Levi to fend for himself for that long. He'd never survive.

"Tell her," Michael grumbled.

"You have the ability to create your own sword. One that will open any dimension you want." I could hear the reluctance in Gabriel's tone. He didn't want me to have this information.

"My own sword..." I let his words sink in. "And you didn't tell me this before because you know any sword I create could be used against you, just like you used the Sword of Angels against me. Was that why you created it?"

Neither of my brothers would look at me, so I took that as an affirmative. *Assholes*. Why did they hate me so much? I'd done nothing to them, nothing, yet still, they plotted to destroy me. I couldn't hate them in return, though. They were my brothers, my family.

I rose to my feet and moved my gaze between the two of them. "And you're positive God isn't here in Heaven? You've searched thoroughly?"

Gabriel shook his head. "We're positive. God is not in Heaven. Why? What are you going to do?"

"I'm going to retrieve Levi and find Dad. In the meantime, I suggest you two do something about healing Heaven."

I didn't wait for their reply. Instead, I turned on my heel and strode out, feeling a sense of satisfaction in the stunned silence I left in my wake. They'd expected a temper tantrum—screaming and yelling. And as much as making that kind of scene appealed to me, I needed to stay focused, for as soon as they'd mentioned creating my own sword, I knew exactly how to do it.

Why hadn't I thought of it before?

THREE

Dacian was waiting by our vehicle when I exited the elevator. He straightened up when he saw me, arching a brow.

"Well?" he prompted.

"Did you know God was missing?"

His stunned expression and mouth hanging open told me all I wanted to know.

"What? Since when? How?" Sliding into the car beside me, he bombarded me with questions I didn't have answers for, but I told him what I did know. That I could get Levi back with my own sword.

He mulled it over as we drove. "How would you create a sword?"

"In the fires of Hell. As soon as they told me, it was like a page-turning. I just knew. It all fell into place. I think this is something Dad always wanted me to know—that it was there, on the edge of my subconscious, only I never needed such a weapon… until now.”

“So you’re going back to Hell?”

I glanced across at him, surprised by the dejected tone in his voice. He was gazing out the window as the vehicle whisked us through Heaven Central and back toward the Pearly Gates.

“Of course.” I continued to watch him, taking in the way his fingers clenched into fists on his knees and the tight set of his jaw. “Come with me,” I said, my voice soft.

These were the words I hadn’t been able to bring myself to say to him all those years ago when I’d first left Heaven. The words that could have saved our relationship. Our love. Instead, I’d left him behind.

His head swiveled, and those stunning blue eyes met mine. “You mean it?”

“As my friend, Dacian.” I placed my hand over his fist. “But yes, I mean it. I can’t leave you here for my brothers to mess with again.”

“They’ll banish me.”

I shook my head. “Nope. You’re on a mission.”

“If you think a mission to rescue a human will save me from banishment, then you don’t know your brothers very well. I don't want to be fallen, Lucy."

"Not a human. God. He's missing. You're a Seraph Angel, Dacian, a warrior. Who better to find him than you? He trusted you to train us. He'll understand that you left Heaven to find him. You won't be fallen." I could see the cogs turning as he thought over my words. "Plus, you won't be alone. You'll be with me. We'll find him together."

"Who gets the credit?" His smirk told me he was joking.

I played along. "You, of course."

He smiled widely. "Deal."

I was glad we were friends again. I'd missed him. I'd blamed myself for not keeping in touch and not knowing what my brothers had done to him. I'd thought I was kind to stay out of his life and let him get on with things without me. The day I'd left, I broke his heart. He knew I'd put my career ahead of our love.

"Why did you?"

For a moment, I wondered if I'd spoken aloud, and I turned to him in surprise. "Why did I what?"

"Tell me not to go to HR?"

I must have been daydreaming while he was talking. "It seemed strange that my brothers hadn't seen you in a while—had sent you on a mission that you didn't return from—and their first instructions were to send you to HR for disciplinary action. They didn't ask why you were with me, or what had happened, or for you to explain yourself. Something was up."

"You have good instincts."

"Do you remember what they did to make you forget me? Have you been to HR before?"

He frowned. "I don't remember *ever* going to HR. I don't remember anything at all, really. Like, if I try to think back on what I've been doing in Heaven these past ten years, I couldn't tell you."

"Weird."

"Right?"

I wondered if my brothers had used the same mind-altering techniques they'd used on Dacian on other angels. That would explain why Earth was in so much trouble. If the Guardian Angels had been brainwashed to not help their charges, it would result in chaos. I itched to investigate further, but my first priority was to rescue Levi and then find Dad. Once God was back in Heaven, he could sort out my brothers and the multitude of problems they'd caused.

Our vehicle came to a stop, and we stepped out.

The gates were still locked, and thousands of people waited dejectedly to get in. They reminded me of the human refugees I'd seen on my monitors, all huddled together, bedraggled, incapable of understanding what was happening to them.

"This worries me," I muttered to Dacian as we pushed our way through the souls, who all pleaded to us for help.

"That you can't help them?"

"Well, yes, but if they are stuck here in limbo for too long, they'll return to Earth as revenants. We can't allow that to happen." A revenant was a soulless entity that could return to Earth to haunt the living.

Dacian cursed, picking up the pace, urgency in his stride. "All the more reason to find God. I can't believe I didn't know he was missing."

"It's not your fault. They fucked with your mind, remember? Or not, I guess." I half laughed at my own joke. Dacian stopped, arms folded over his chest, and stared at me. "Okay, so it wasn't that funny."

Dacian shook his head. "No, you idiot, that's not why I stopped. We're going to Hell, yes? I don't know the way."

"Oh, right. Of course." My cheeks warmed with

embarrassment, something that hadn't happened since my early days training with Dacian. Clearing my throat, I held out my hand to him. "This way."

"What is *he* doing here?"

Arching a brow, I studied Ashliel, noting her narrowed green eyes and the hands-on-hips stance, flaming red hair dancing and flickering around her shoulders. Ashliel was my second-in-command, and she was awesome, but she was also pissed, which aroused my curiosity. Why would she be annoyed I'd brought Dacian to Hell?

"He's helping me." Keeping my voice neutral, I looked at Dacian, who was watching Ashliel with a goofy grin on his face. *Wait.* "Have you two met before?" I asked.

"No," they said in unison, but no matter how much they denied it, my senses were tingling. Something was up with these two, but we were on a tight time frame, and I didn't have time to stand around wondering about it.

"Dacian can fill you in while I pop down to the pit." I was already halfway across the floor, heading toward the elevator that would deliver me from my offices atop Hell HQ to Hell's one and only fiery pit.

"Wait!"

Ashliel hurried along behind me. I glanced at her over my shoulder. She was holding her electronic clipboard and had begun to rattle off questions.

"We're almost at full capacity. We need to escalate our expansion plans. Do you want me to get started on that?"

"Yes."

She typed something into her clipboard, then said, "A soul that ascended has returned to us."

That caught my attention. An ascended soul, returned? It wasn't possible. I told Ashliel as much.

"Maybe, but it's true nonetheless." Her green eyes met mine. "Any idea why?"

"Possibly because Dad is missing," I said. "That's why Dacian is here, to help me find him. But first, I need to create the Sword of Souls."

"The what of what?"

"No time to explain." The elevator doors slid open, and I stepped inside, turning and placing my hand on her chest to stop her from following. "No. Dacian will fill you in. I trust you to make the right decisions about this place. Yes, to expansion. You know how to field the requests from the sinners. I have every confidence in you. But right now, my priorities are making the sword, retrieving Levi, and finding Dad."

The doors closed, cutting off her response, and I was whisked down to the pit. The pit was reserved for the most heinous of sinners, and as I walked the gangway suspended over it, the heat hit me, then the screams, followed by the stench. I didn't like the pit, but that was the whole point, wasn't it? No one was meant to like the pit.

Since God created Hell, not a single soul had escaped the pit nor repented their sins. Beyond the superficial screaming and cursing, none of them had changed. Deep down inside, their souls were tainted. There was no saving them. I remembered the argument I'd had with Dad—wouldn't it be more compassionate to extinguish their souls rather than condemn them to burn in the pit for all eternity? But God had a plan, and this, apparently, was part of it.

Stopping in the center of the walkway, I spread my wings, closed my eyes, and swan-dived into the firestorm below. My clothes burst into flames, then turn to ashes, but my body remained unharmed. The souls around me writhed as I continued down, deeper and deeper until I reached the very bottom of the ocean of fire. Everything around me burned a kaleidoscope of red, yellow, and orange.

Crouching, I scooped up a pile of ash in one hand and, with my wing, I sliced open my opposite palm. Blood dripped down, mixing with the ash. Closing my eyes, I began the chant that would bring the Sword of Souls into creation—words that had been locked inside me for all this time, waiting to be released.

The ash swirled in my palm, twisting up into the air, mingling with my blood. It glowed pale blue, then white, as the blade began to take shape. My fingers closed around the hilt, and I was almost overwhelmed by the connection I felt with it. We were one, the sword and I. For a moment, I stood in the flames of Hell, the sword raised over my head as I reveled in its power.

Then I sneezed and almost peed myself, bringing me back to reality. I didn't have time to stand around here basking in my awesomeness. I had a job to do.

Flying up through the pit, the sword in my hand, I landed gracefully on the walkway and made my way back to the elevator. Ashliel and Dacian were waiting for me up in my offices. I hoped Ashliel hadn't singed him. I still didn't understand why she didn't want him here. It couldn't be because he was an angel—she was an angel, too, after all. I'd recruited her from Heaven myself.

"So that's the Sword of Souls," Ashliel breathed when I returned, her eyes on the blade. It no longer glowed blue and white but crackled with flame.

"Er, Lucy?" Dacian sounded like he was choking.

"What's up?"

"Your clothes?" he muttered, looking at everything but me.

"What about them?"

I glanced down just as he replied, "You're not wearing any!"

With a laugh, I materialized a new outfit, a black, skin-tight pantsuit. If I was going to act the superhero, I was sure as hell going to dress the part. Sliding the sword into the holster at my hip, I said, "I need a superhero name."

Ashliel groaned, shaking her head. "You don't think being Lucifer, Queen of Hell, is enough?"

"I want something cool. You know, like Spiderman. Or Wonder Woman. Have you noticed there aren't that many female superheroes?"

"Are you serious?" Dacian muttered.

"Deadly."

"What about Levi?" he asked, waving a hand around.

"I can't call myself Levi. That's Levi's name," I pointed out. Then I realized what he was getting at. "Oh! You mean, stop standing around choosing superhero names and go rescue Levi? Right?"

"Yes." Was he grinding his jaw? I shot Ashliel a look, but she was watching Dacian intently.

"Okay, then, let's go," I said. "We can brainstorm names on the way."

FOUR

The Sword of Souls cut through the veil between dimensions like a hot knife through butter. I tossed a satisfied grin over my shoulder at Dacian before stepping through into the Xoelax dimension.

"Where do we start looking?" Dacian asked as he stepped through behind me and surveyed the bleak landscape that greeted us.

"I can feel him."

As soon as I'd stepped into this plane, I sensed the connection between Levi and me, like a cord flexing between us. I hadn't been able to feel that connection since Levi had been taken, yet I'd known he wasn't dead, for surely I would have felt the severing of our bond. No, the connection had been temporarily blocked but not severed. Now I just needed to follow it, and Levi would be at the other end.

"So, you're bonded then?" Dacian's voice was rough like he'd been chewing gravel. I glanced at him. He couldn't still harbor feelings for me, could he? Not after all this time?

I shrugged. "I guess." Not an outright lie, which I couldn't do. But I could dance around the truth.

"With a human." His observation was more to himself than to me.

"Love is love. It knows no boundaries," I reminded him. That had been one of Dad's mottos, among a host of others. The man had a motto for every occasion.

"And yet—" He cut himself off, and I looked at him speculatively. Where was he going with this?

"And yet...what?" The tone of my voice had changed. I was getting pissed off. Why was Dacian so intent on belittling my relationship with Levi? If he wasn't careful, I'd clip his wings with my new sword.

"When you left me, you told me a relationship between us wouldn't work because of the distance between Heaven and Hell. The boundaries." The hurt in his voice was unmistakable, and I winced. I had said that. But I'd said it thousands of years ago. It was long past time for Dacian to get over himself.

"I was young and naïve, Dacian," I said impatiently. "I'm sorry I hurt you. I truly am. But that was a long time ago. A very, very long time ago. It has no bearing on the here and now or on my relationship with Levi."

"I'd forgotten until my memories came back. So while you may have moved on and this is all ancient history to you, for me, it's real, it's raw, and it's fresh."

Fuck! I could feel Dacian's pain, but Levi's pull was a distraction, and I was torn. Stay and talk about feelings with Dacian? Or rescue Levi? Okay, it was a no-brainer, but I still felt like a bitch for hurting Dacian. Again.

"Let's finish up here, and we'll talk about this later, okay?" My words came out harsher than I anticipated. Dacian stiffened. His face went blank, and he nodded once.

"I'll guard the portal and make sure no one gets through. You go find Levi." His voice was devoid of emotion. I was messing this up big time, but I couldn't afford to wait any longer. I could feel Levi's agitation. I knew he was in trouble. I would never forgive myself if something happened to him while I was having a deep and meaningful discussion with Dacian.

Without another word, I spread my wings and flew across the desolate landscape. To my left was an outcropping of rocks, and I veered toward it, my connection with Levi growing stronger the closer I got. And then I spotted him, running at full speed, a horde of Xoelaxians in pursuit.

Swooping in fast and low, I scooped him up in both arms, holding him close against my body. I zoomed high into the air, twisting and turning to avoid the arrows the Xoelaxians began shooting at us. Levi was panting, breathless but alive.

"What kept you?" he wheezed.

"I couldn't get through the portal," I explained, "so I took a quick trip to Heaven to get some help. Are you okay?"

"I'm fine." But something in his voice told me I had another male on my hands whose feathers were well and truly ruffled. *Great.*

"I'm sorry you got taken and that I couldn't come for you sooner." My apology was sincere, and I pressed my lips to his neck.

He jerked away. "It's been weeks, Lucy."

"No, it hasn't. It's been a couple of hours at most," I argued.

"Bullshit," he spat. "Look at me. Do I look like I've been here for a couple of hours?"

I glanced at his clothing, torn and dirty, and took in his long, filthy hair. I couldn't see his face clearly, but there was a beard now covering his jaw.

"Shit. Fuck! I'm sorry! Time must move differently here. I came as quickly as I could, I swear. I had to get help."

He kept quiet while I told him of my trip to Heaven, the confrontation with my brothers, the news that dad was missing, and the subsequent creation of the Sword of Souls. Slowly, he relaxed in my arms, and I was relieved he believed I hadn't left him here to rot.

Dacian was waiting for us at the portal. He greeted Levi with a slap on the back and grunted, "Glad you're still alive."

We hurried through the portal. It wasn't until I'd sealed it with the sword that I relaxed. Levi was back —back on Earth, where he belonged. I put the strange vibe I was getting from him down to the fact that he'd been trapped in another dimension for weeks. That would rattle anyone, especially if death was imminent. The thought that he could have died filled my mind, and my eyes soon filled with tears. I'd almost lost him. The relief that he was standing here in front of me now was overwhelming, and I threw myself into his arms, uncaring that Dacian muttered, "Oh, for fuck's sake," and stomped away.

Levi returned my embrace, pressing his face into the curve of my neck, breathing deeply. Shivers danced over my skin, covering me in goosebumps.

"I want you so damn much," he whispered, "but not here. Fucking in a cemetery isn't on my list of things to do. At least not today."

I shivered, anticipation making my knees weak. "Let's go home."

Pressing myself to his chest, smiling in wicked delight when his arms wrapped around me tightly, I extended my wings, and within seconds we were standing at his door.

Mr. Meow greeted us, weaving between our legs and threatening to trip us. I bent to rub his ears, squealing in surprise when Levi stepped up behind me, clasping my hips and pressing hard against me.

"I like this," he growled. "But..."

"But?" I questioned, twisting my head to look at him over my shoulder.

"I need to get cleaned up first."

"What if I like it dirty?" I couldn't stop the words tumbling from my mouth.

"Oh, you're still going to get it dirty, don't you worry." He slapped my butt before releasing me, disappearing into the bathroom before I could respond.

"I need the sword back."

Dacian's demand caught me by surprise, and I squealed, spinning to see him standing in the living room, arms crossed over his chest. Oh, he was pissed, and given what he'd probably just witnessed, I couldn't blame him.

"Right." Stepping back, I rapped on the bathroom door. "Levi? Dacian needs the sword back." I'd noticed the Sword of Angels strapped to Levi's belt when I rescued him. The bathroom door swung open so fast I stepped back in surprise.

"I don't think so." Levi's eyes were hard and cold, and his hand rested protectively on the hilt of the sword.

"That—" Dacian nodded his head at the sword. "—is the Sword of Angels, and it doesn't belong on Earth. I'm taking it with me."

"You gave it to me. I'm keeping it," Levi shot back.

"I let you borrow it. Now it's time to give it back."

"Boys," I warned. The air was thick with

testosterone. The last thing I needed was these two fighting.

"Don't fret, Lucy," Dacian sneered, "I won't hurt your boyfriend."

"As if you could!" Levi protested, starting to withdraw the sword from his belt loop. Oh, good grief, what were they doing? *Idiots.*

Holding out his hand, Dacian muttered something. The sword ripped free of Levi's grasp, flying across the room and into Dacian's hands.

"What the hell?" Levi yelled.

"Sword of Angels," Dacian smirked. "I'm an Angel. You're not. Remember?"

"You're an asshole." Levi's voice was laced with fury, and I looked at him in surprise. Where was this coming from?

Dacian shrugged, a self-satisfied look on his face. "Maybe. But the sword wasn't meant for you, just like she's not meant for you."

"Dacian!"

Before I could say anything further, he spread his wings and disappeared. Rubbing a hand over my face, I struggled to get a grip on what had just happened. The two of them fighting over the sword, then Dacian's dig about me? I was going to have to sort things out with him, I realized. No more tiptoeing around his feelings and worrying about hurting him. I couldn't stand by and let him sabotage my relationship with Levi because he was jealous.

"I think you should go," Levi said.

"What? Why?" I spun, my heart freezing in my chest. I'd just found Levi. Why would I leave? Plus, we'd just been about to get intimate. I had no intention of going anywhere.

"I'm tired."

Looking now at his drawn face and empty eyes, I berated myself for being so selfish. He honestly did look awful. Not only was his skin covered with a layer of dirt, but he also had bruises and scratches. He'd lost weight, sported a scraggly beard, and his hair was a red hot mess.

"Let me help." Cupping his face in my hands, I smiled softly when he didn't pull away. He was skittish, and I couldn't blame him. He'd endured what no human should have to endure. He needed time to adjust to being back home, and I had to respect that. I sent my healing power into him, and before my eyes, his cheeks filled out, his injuries healed, his hair smoothed itself out, and there was a sexy five o'clock shadow where his beard had been.

"Thanks, but—" He wouldn't meet my eyes,

instead stepping back into the bathroom. "I still want to be alone. I want a long, hot shower—alone. I want to sleep—alone." The emphasis on the word "alone" stung. Not to mention, his whole demeanor confused me. He was all over me one minute, then pushing me away the next. I wasn't used to hot and cold, didn't know how to take it. But I loved Levi, and I had to respect his wishes. After what he'd been through, it was the least I could do.

"Okay. Just...call me? When you're ready?"

"Call you how? You live in Hell, remember? It's not like there's a phone line between here and there." His sarcasm was so uncharacteristic that I took a step back. What was wrong with him?

"Use the psychic link. Like you did the first time you contacted me. I'll hear you."

"Fine." The bathroom door slammed, leaving me stunned. This was not the homecoming I had envisioned. Not knowing what to do with myself but not wanting to anger Levi further, I gave Mr. Meow one last fuss before returning to Hell.

FIVE

"Back so soon?"

Dacian's taunt was the final straw. I hadn't been expecting to find him waiting in my office, and his presence, along with his sarcastic dig, grated on my nerves.

"What did you do?" I accused, hands on my hips, eyes narrowed.

"What did I do? Oh, that's rich."

"Why are you all acting so crazy?" I cried.

Dacian was jealous as if I had been cheating on him. Levi was just being plain weird, but I attributed that to weeks he'd spent constantly on guard and in fear of his life. He'd need time to adjust. But Dacian? Okay, so his memories had only just returned—or so he said—but it wasn't like him to act like such a douche.

"Maybe you're the crazy one," he said.

That was it. I'd reached my limit. I flew at him, punched him in the jaw, and followed him to the floor, intent on unleashing as much pain as possible. How dare he come to my home and treat me like this?

We tussled on the floor in an undignified brawl for several minutes. I heard Ashliel laughing and clapping and dancing with glee at the spectacle we were making, but I couldn't rein it in. I was pissed off and fed up, and I was going to take it out on Dacian. He clearly felt the same way. His fist caught my head, snapping it back. Pain radiated from my jaw.

"Ow. Fuck." I toppled, cradling my face. He'd broken bones. I winced as I channeled my magic to heal them.

"Shit." Dacian was beside me in a second, his face contrite. "I'm sorry. Fuck, I didn't mean to hurt you."

"Yes, you did, just like I meant to hurt you. Come on, Dacian, don't start lying now. This is us...remember?"

"That's just it. I remember loving you. And you

leaving. *That's* what I remember." He sat with his knees drawn up, arms resting on them, head bowed. "I don't remember grieving or healing."

"It's been, like, thousands of years since then," I whispered, feeling his pain. It radiated from him, and I wanted desperately to ease it. He'd been through this already. It was unfair he had to go through it again.

"My brain knows what you say is true, but my emotions? They haven't caught up."

"How can I help?" I moved to my knees, my hand on his arm.

He blew out a heavy sigh. "I don't know. It's in my head, right? Can you..."

"Get in your head?" I guessed where he was going.

He nodded. "You're the only one I trust. Things still aren't right up here." He tapped his temple. "I need everything sorted. I need to be on the top of my game to find God."

"I guess I can try?"

"Just promise me you won't mess with anything, Lucy. Don't change anything. Not to save my feelings or make me feel better. I just need the truth. I need my life back."

"I promise I'll just unblock whatever is blocking you."

"Oh, man. You two spoil all the fun." Ashliel flounced away, apparently disappointed that our fight was over.

Dacian and I grinned at each other, then he jumped to his feet, holding out his hand to haul me up.

"Let's get comfortable, shall we?" He headed to the sofa, and I followed. Taking a seat at one end, I indicated he should lay down with his head in my lap.

"Thanks for trusting me with this." I looked down into his blue eyes, tried to ignore the love I could see blazing in them. He'd be over that soon enough. I wondered if he'd loved again after me. He probably had, for Dacian had a big heart and was a good man. What had become of her, his latest love? Had he forgotten her as well? Was she waiting for him somewhere, wondering what had happened?

"Hey, what's that expression for?" He touched my cheek, bringing me back to the present.

"Nothing." Clearing my throat, I flexed my fingers and then placed one palm on his forehead. "Let's do this. Close your eyes."

I concentrated on the connection between us,

where my flesh touched his, and followed it from the tips of my fingers to his forehead, then deeper, along the superhighways of his mind. And as I moved through his mind, I found them—plain, everyday doors, only some of them were crossed with yellow tape. Locked. Approaching each of those doors, I tore down the tape and flung them open, letting his memories loose.

It didn't take long, but it was exhausting, for I felt each memory as it fled its prison, as it burst through me and into him, to find its rightful place. They were a kaleidoscope of images, moving much too fast for me to make sense of them. I was actually grateful for that. To see and know all of his innermost thoughts would be way too intrusive.

Finally, I was done. Removing my hand from his forehead, I opened my eyes to look down at him, only to find him out cold. I lifted his head and eased myself out from under him, leaving him to sleep it off. I sent up a silent prayer that I'd done the right thing.

STANDING BENEATH MY WATERFALL SHOWER, I let the warm water flow over me, trying not to think of

Levi. I failed. Every minute or so, I was reaching out to our connection, feeling for the bond, and while reassured that he was there, he also wasn't calling for me. I was wondering why, but I was also hurt.

Me. Lucifer. Crying in the shower because my feelings were hurt. A tongue of flame licked from my fingers, and I curled my fingers into a fist to contain it.

"Keep your emotions under control," I whispered to myself.

"I say let them out and have at it," Ashliel commented from her perch on the granite bench in my bathroom.

"What, and destroy everyone in my path because I'm having a temper tantrum that things aren't going my way?"

"Why not?" She tossed her hair over her shoulder, the flames following a nanosecond later.

I laughed. "You're such a bloodthirsty little thing."

Ashliel and I were as different as chalk and cheese. Whereas I delivered punishment and inflicted pain because it was my job, I didn't enjoy it. I often felt bad about it. But not Ashliel. She enjoyed it, even reveled in it. She made the perfect second-in-command.

Turning off the shower, I stepped out, accepting the towel Ashliel handed me.

"You should do it," she said, head cocked to one side.

"What, unleash my temper?"

"No, silly." She laughed. "Go see Levi."

"He said he wanted to be alone," I protested, wrapping the towel around myself and knotting it between my breasts.

"And he has been alone. You're worried he hasn't called? Go find out why. You fought so damn hard to get him back, and now he's blowing you off? You should get those answers...you deserve them."

"You're right."

Buoyed by her encouragement, I dried off and tossed the towel at her, striding naked into my dressing area, where I surveyed row after row of dresses, pants, and pantsuits. I didn't necessarily need a wardrobe full of clothes considering I could summon any outfit I wanted. It was pure ego that had me standing before my impressive collection, but I refused to apologize for it. We all have our foibles. I settled on a long dress that brushed around my ankles, cinched in tight at my waist, and cupped my breasts in a becoming halter neck. In red, of course, to complement my dark hair.

"You look stunning," Ashliel said.

She always had been my number one cheerleader, and I appreciated her more than ever now, especially since Levi's rejection had bruised my ego. But had he really rejected me? He'd asked for some alone time. Did that count as rejection?

Yes, a tiny voice answered. *Because he'd primed you for an epic love-making session, had been rubbing up against you, then he sent you away.*

Tired of my own inner monologue, I gave Ashliel a quick hug before materializing in Levi's apartment. Mr. Meow greeted me immediately, purring and rubbing against my legs.

"Hey, boy." I crouched, running my hand over his silky head and down his body. He purred in approval. "So where's your dad, eh? Is he sleeping?"

"Trying to," Levi grumbled from the sofa. Peering over it, I saw him sprawled on his back, a towel tied around his hips, one arm thrown over his eyes.

"Sorry if I woke you." Suddenly full of doubt, I backed away toward the door. I shouldn't have come. He'd specifically asked for some space, and I'd blatantly ignored his request. If our roles had been reversed, I'd be annoyed too.

"It's okay. I'm sorry, too," he said.

That stopped me in my tracks. "You are?"

"Yeah." He removed the arm from over his eyes and sat up. "I'm sorry I asked you to leave. I wish I hadn't."

"You do?" I couldn't keep the delight from my voice, and I winced a little at my own enthusiasm when I saw his lip curl in a smirk.

"I was just...overwhelmed?"

It was more of a question than a statement, and I crossed to him, perching on the side of the sofa as I clasped one of his hands in mine. "A lot has happened. And for you, a lot of time went by. No wonder you thought I'd abandoned you. I'd never do that to you, Levi. Ever."

"I know." He squeezed my hand, his hazel eyes intent. "I did things, Lucy. Bad things."

Sucking in a breath, I whispered, "Like what?"

"I killed a man. I killed Zuska."

"In self-defense?"

He nodded, not meeting my eyes. "But...I think he tricked me into it. I think he wanted me to do it."

"Why?"

"To alert the rest of his tribe that I was there. As soon as his blood hit the ground, it alerted them. They hunted me from that point on."

"That's an extreme way to get his tribe's

attention. To sacrifice himself." I frowned. Surely Zuska could have taken Levi to the tribe instead? It made no sense. Unless… "Do you think he felt he'd failed in his mission to permanently take up residence on Earth and open the portal? Did you get a sense that, to him, failure was not an option? That death was the only alternative?"

Levi was silent for a moment, digesting my words. Then he shrugged. "I honestly don't know. We didn't really talk. It happened right after we'd come back through the portal."

I rested my palm on his cheek and leaned in close. "Levi, you did what you had to do to survive. You were in a realm not meant for humans. You'll be forgiven."

"Is that what you think? That I'm worried God won't forgive me?" He sounded surprised.

"Aren't you?"

"No. I mean, you're living proof that Heaven and Hell do exist, but…I don't know. I just…"

"What?"

The silence stretched between us, and I wondered what was going on behind his gorgeous eyes. I had no sense of what he was thinking or feeling. Then the blank look was gone. His eyes twinkled, his lip curled, and with a whispered

"Come here," he cupped the back of my neck and pulled me to him. The second his lips touched mine, all thought fled. Whatever I'd been worrying about was gone. It was just the two of us, and the heat of his mouth, the slide of his tongue, the shiver that traveled the length of my spine and pooled in my belly.

We could have been anywhere. Our surroundings didn't matter anymore. There was nothing else in the world but Levi—his arms around me, his breath on my face, his lips grazing mine, his eyes drinking in my face. He lowered his mouth again with a low moan in his throat. The sound sent an electric current through my veins. I couldn't get close enough. I wanted more than his mouth on mine, so much more.

I heard fabric tearing, but who needed clothes anyway? Certainly not Levi and me. I'd be thrilled to be naked with him for the rest of our days. His hands were everywhere, my skin sensitive under his touch. It was hard to focus on anything with such intense sensations pulling my attention to a million different places in my body. Places he explored with a thoroughness that stole my breath.

I wasn't sure if it was the relief at having him back and safe that amplified our love-making, for each brush of his fingers left a path of fire that I reveled in. This moment seared itself into my brain. Ours. Ours alone. I nipped at him with my teeth, soothing the bite with my tongue, running my hands over his shoulders, reveling in the chuckle I felt vibrate through him and into me.

He was my everything.

SIX

I woke to the sensation of heat. A lot of it. Rolling onto my back, I checked that I hadn't inadvertently set the room on fire, but there were no flames in sight. Just Levi asleep next to me, radiating an enormous amount of heat. Worried, I placed my palm on his forehead. Shit, he was burning up.

"What is it?" He mumbled, cracking open one eye to peer at me.

"You've got a fever. How do you feel?" Worry tinged my voice. Had he brought back an infection from Xoelax?

"What? No way! I'm fine." He bounced out of bed, gloriously naked, and strode into the bathroom. I watched the magnificence of his muscled back, tight ass, and long, lean legs before letting my hand drop to where he'd been laying on the bed only moments earlier. Definitely hot. What was up with him if he wasn't ill?

His head appeared around the door frame, and he crooked his finger. "Coming?"

The promise in his voice had me leaping from the bed and into his arms in record time. Our naked flesh collided, and I reveled in it, in the way every nerve ending sprang to life, from the tips of my toes to the top of my head. Threading his fingers through my hair, he angled my head the way he wanted it and kissed me. He kissed me like I'd wanted to be kissed my entire life—with everything he had. That kiss told me he was mine, and I was his. That kiss touched my very soul. It branded me. My head swam with it, my knees buckled, and I sagged against him, consumed by him.

"You're so hot," I whispered when his lips left mine to explore across my jaw and down my neck.

"So are you, babe." He nipped, then soothed the sting with his tongue. He was doing crazy things to me, things that made my blood heat in my veins.

"No, seriously. You're fucking hot." I placed my palms on his chest and pushed, putting some distance between us. "As in, you have a temperature. Your skin feels feverish."

"I'm not sick, I promise." He pulled me back against him, his arm a hard band around my waist. "I want you so damn much."

The way he growled the words had me coming undone, unable to focus, no longer worried about his heat. Instead, I wanted more of it. I wanted his warmth wrapped around me. If he was going to go up in flames, I'd join the inferno, and we'd burn together.

***

"You two finally decided to come up for air, I see." Dacian was sitting at the breakfast bar, a cup of steaming coffee in front of him as he flicked through a newspaper.

"When did you get here?" I couldn't wipe the smile from my face. This morning with Levi had my skin tingling in all the right places.

"A little while ago. You were busy. I made coffee." He nodded to the coffee pot, and I happily made my way to it, pouring myself a cup.

I noticed no jealous undertones in his voice and

prayed my little foray into his brain had worked. "How are you feeling?" I ventured.

"Good. I feel good."

"So…" I shuffled my feet, feeling awkward. "Those feelings from before? Gone?" I winced at the hopeful pitch in my voice, feeling like a bitch.

He grinned at me and winked. "Yup. You're history. Ancient, history."

"Not so much of the ancient, if you don't mind." Taking a sip of my coffee, I closed my eyes to savor the aromatic goodness. The humans had done well with this discovery. I'd been sneaking off to Earth for some time to stock up on my coffee bean supply.

"Hey." Levi strode in, barefoot in jeans and a blue button-down shirt, hair damp from the shower.

"Feeling better?" Dacian asked him. "You looked like a wreck yesterday."

"Much better, thanks."

"Does he feel hot to you?" I pushed Levi toward Dacian, and both men looked at me, Dacian with surprise, Levi with annoyance.

"I told you," he said, "I'm fine."

"I feel heat, but it's coming from you," Dacian said to me, returning his attention to the newspaper. "You are Lucifer, after all. I'd expect some residual heat from Hell to radiate off of you."

"Ha!" Levi crowed. "It's been you all along!"

Frowning, I looked down into my cup, searching its dark depths for I didn't know what. Could it be true? Was the heat coming off Levi's skin a reflection of mine? Was it simply radiating back at me?

Levi busied himself in the kitchen making breakfast, and I took a seat next to Dacian, content to stay out of the way.

"So." Dacian folded the paper and put it to one side, swiveling to face me. "What's the plan for finding God? Any idea where we should start?"

"Gah." Where was one supposed to begin the search for a missing God? I'd been so consumed with finding Levi that I hadn't given a whole lot of thought to Dad's situation, but now it was unavoidable.

"Prayer?" Levi suggested over the sizzle of bacon.

I let out a weary sigh, consumed by guilt. "From what I've seen here, God's been ignoring prayers for a long, long time. I should have realized something was up. I should have checked."

"Hey!" Dacian nudged my knee with his. "This isn't your fault! None of us had a clue. We thought he was just off doing his thing. Whatever his thing is."

"Well, you had your mind wiped, anyway, so there's no way you would have been aware."

"I have an idea."

Levi turned to us and slid a plate piled high with bacon, scrambled eggs, and fried tomatoes in front of me. I had to wipe my chin to make sure I hadn't drooled. Cooking was a skill I lacked, and I was very quickly developing a love of human food—or, more accurately, food prepared by a particular human.

"Oh?" I said around a mouthful of the fluffiest scrambled eggs I'd ever tasted.

Levi nodded. "Use me. I can try to channel him. All I need is an object to use for channeling, and I stand a reasonable chance of locating him."

I thought for a moment. "Can you use me as the object? I'm his creation. I'm made from his blood."

He shrugged, shoveling food into his mouth. "An inanimate object is better, but I could try if you want."

"We can go to Heaven and retrieve something that belongs to him," Dacian said.

We could, but I suspected my brothers had Dad's house on lockdown. Anyway, I had a better idea.

"The sword will probably work."

Dacian frowned. "The Sword of Souls? But you only just created it. It's yours, not God's."

"It's a long shot, yes, but it's made of my DNA. Which is part of Dad's DNA. It could work, couldn't it, Levi?"

"We can try it and see," Levi said.

"Oh, damn, no, it won't work." I was annoyed that I'd overlooked the obvious. "Only Dad and I can hold it. It's made from us and bound to us. You won't be able to touch it."

"Let's try it and see. I could hold the Sword of Angels with no problems at all. In fact, that sword got passed around to all sorts, including ghosts. You might be surprised."

Levi's words alarmed me, for he was right. Heaven's sword *had* been held by many, belying the commonly-held belief that it could only be wielded by God and his chosen one. Had the knowledge I'd downloaded about my own sword been wrong? Out of date? Or had my brothers found a way around the rules?

"Okay." The sword materialized in my hand, and I placed it on the kitchen counter. "Just be careful, please."

"I won't damage it," Levi assured me.

"It's not the sword I'm worried about." I rolled my shoulders, trying to relieve the tension building there. Why was I so angsty all of a sudden? The air felt thicker somehow. It was harder to breathe. Yet when I looked at Levi and Dacian, they were perfectly fine. Was I having a panic attack? My chest grew tighter, and I placed a hand over my chest to calm my racing heart. What the hell was going on?

"Here goes." Levi closed his hand around the hilt of the sword. I scrunched my eyes shut, afraid to see his hand burst into flames, and held my breath as I waited for his pained screams. When only silence filled the room, I cracked open an eye and took a peek. Levi stood calmly with the sword in his hand. No pain. No flames—except those dancing along the blade. *What. The. Hell?*

"Getting anything?" Dacian enquired curiously.

I looked between the two of them. How could they be so calm? Didn't they know the enormity of this? Or, again, had I gotten it all wrong? Humans were not supposed to wield the Sword of Souls— they absolutely, irrevocably, could not touch it. I'd read the inscription on the blade. Even Dacian shouldn't be able to hold it. Yet Levi stood with it firmly in his grasp, with no ill effects. A headache started to thrum behind my eyes, and I pinched the bridge of my nose.

"Yeah, I'm getting a sense of him," Levi muttered.

My head shot up, and I leaned forward. "So he's alive?"

Levi nodded. "Yes. Alive."

"Where? Where is he?"

"I'm trying. Hang on." Levi closed his eyes, his face a picture of concentration. I held my breath until Dacian nudged me and whispered at me to breathe.

"Damn, lost it." Levi's eyes opened and landed on me. "He's definitely alive, but I couldn't pinpoint where he is. I could only see darkness. A lot of darkness."

"Do we know if he's in Heaven, at least?" Dacian asked.

Levi shrugged. "Couldn't tell what dimension. Sorry."

"Well, he's alive." I was as surprised as anyone at the wobble in my voice. I hadn't allowed myself to entertain the idea that Dad might be dead, and now that I knew he wasn't, a wave of emotion hit me. Hard.

Levi wrapped an arm around my shoulder and

pulled me in close. "We'll find him. It'll be okay," he said soothingly, and I nodded.

"Okay, let's regroup," Dacian said, taking charge. I gave him a watery smile. This was his thing. He was good at this. "We know God is alive. We also know he's missing—missing in that he hasn't been seen in Heaven, or anywhere, for millennia. We also know that Heaven is deteriorating. The Pearly Gates are locked. Buildings are decaying. My question is, would things be falling apart if God was still in Heaven?"

"We need to get to the archives," I said. The archives held the complete history of Heaven, Earth, and Hell. "If we could pinpoint why Heaven is crumbling, maybe that will give us a clue as to where he is. Or at least a realm we can start searching in!"

"Let's do it," Dacian said to me, extending his wings, ready to leave.

"Hold on just a minute." Levi's voice rang out, a hardness I hadn't heard before coating his words. "Where she goes, I go."

"Heaven isn't for living mortals," Dacian said dismissively.

"Neither was Xoelax, but I went there and survived it."

He had a point. Dacian looked between the two of us and shrugged. "It's your call, Lucy."

Levi took hold of my shoulders and turned me to face him, looking intently into my face. "I am not losing you again," he murmured, his eyes burning with passion. "Wherever you go, I will find a way to follow. Might as well make it easier on all of us and take me with you."

Who could resist? Certainly not me.

"Okay," I whispered, choked with emotion. "Let's do this."

SEVEN

Dressed in my new favorite outfit—a black catsuit—and with Levi's hand clasped firmly in mine, I took us to Heaven. Dacian had gone on ahead, and as I landed, I could see him in the middle of an altercation with my brothers.

"No. Absolutely not. We tolerated her previous visit, even gave her information that was to her benefit. She can consider herself banished." Gabriel was inches from Dacian's face, arms waving around. Quite frankly, he was making a spectacle of himself. The displaced souls gathered around the Pearly Gates with great interest, and angels already in heaven stopped to see what the fuss was all about.

"You don't have that authority." I interrupted

Gabriel's tirade, slipping through the gap in the gate Dacian had left for me. I kept a tight hold on Levi. I was pushing my luck, even bringing him here.

"In God's absence, I do," Gabriel said.

"Says who? Is it in the scrolls?"

"What do you know of the scrolls?" Michael sneered, and I really wanted to wipe that look right off his face. With my fist.

Dragging in a calming breath, I slowly exhaled before answering. "Quite a lot, actually. We're heading there now. Maybe I'll look up who is next in command when God isn't in residence. Since that has never happened before, I'm not sure such provisions have been established, but hey, let's check, just to be sure."

I caught the look my brothers exchanged and wondered for the millionth time what they were up to. Yes, they wanted Earth for themselves, but why? Of all the universes, and all the galaxies, and all the planets, why Earth? And why were they going to such extremes?

Gabriel looked Levi up and down, the contempt clear on his face. "I take it you're the human she was so desperate to retrieve from Xoelax?"

Levi gave a nod.

"You have our sword," Michael said. "Hand it over. Now."

"Oh, so now we're allowed in? Because we have your sword? The one you were careless enough to lose?" I taunted, unable to keep from grinning.

"You're as annoying as always," Michael grumbled, his gaze darting between Levi and me. "I suggest you hand the sword over now before anyone gets hurt."

"Seriously? You're making threats now?"

Gabriel stepped toward Levi, and I moved in front of him, blocking his way.

"You don't get to touch him," I growled.

"You don't make the rules." Gabriel shoved my shoulder, and I staggered before regaining my balance.

Levi bristled behind me. I could feel his heat against my back, could feel the wave of anger accompanying it. "I don't need you to protect me, Lucy," he said.

"Oh?" Gabriel laughed. "You think you can take me, human?"

"I'm cleaning up your mess, so if you don't mind..." I pushed Gabriel aside, intent on getting to the hovercar I could see waiting, but he grabbed my arm and flung it away.

"I do mind," he spat.

"The chaos you're unleashing on Earth, unchecked, is all on you," I accused.

"That's where you're wrong. This is your fault. It always has been."

While I tried to make sense of that accusation, he threw a punch. I caught it and, curling my fingers over his knuckles, pushed with all my might, sending him skidding across the ground. Righting himself, Gabriel launched at me, but I was ready. Fists flying, we cut into each other.

Spitting blood, I yelled, "You think I want to be here?" Punch. "If it wasn't for you, I'd be home now." Punch. "Instead, I'm here, sorting out your mess." Punch.

Gabriel got beneath my defenses, and his fist connected with my jaw, snapping my head back. I returned the favor, blow for blow, until we were flying through the air, our path obstructed by the hovercar. We slammed into it with a sickening crunch, and glass rained down on us. I was tiring, but so was Gabriel. His clothing was torn and filthy, blood smeared across his face and knuckles. I suspected I looked no better.

"You're here because of your precious human." Gabriel spat out a gob of blood, laughing. "Now I understand what this tantrum is all about. It's about Levi."

"Don't you say his name," I warned, wiping my nose on my forearm.

"I mean, I don't blame you, sister," Gabriel taunted. "These humans can be wild in the sack."

Grabbing him by the lapels of his jacket, I head-butted him. "Levi has nothing to do with this. You gave the ghosts the Sword of Angels. If you wanted me dead, you should have had the balls to do it yourself."

Gabriel staggered back, hand to his nose. "Oh, please, you're the one playing games, twisting things to suit your own needs. You have Hell. Now you want Heaven. It's not going to happen." Gabriel threw another punch. As it collided with my face, my head jerked back, and the vertebrae in my neck cracked.

"I don't even know what you're talking about." Punch.

"You always were a lousy liar." Punch.

I paused for a moment to catch my breath. "That's just it, Gabriel. I can't lie."

"ENOUGH!" Michael yelled, hands on his hips.

We ignored him.

"You don't understand the full picture." Gabriel swung again.

I ducked and threw my own punch. "Then explain it to me."

"Stop hitting me! You have a tendency to get emotional about things." I punched him again, but he blocked it, muttering, "Case in point."

"You don't care about anyone other than yourself unless they can be of use to you," I accused.

We tumbled together, fists swinging, droplets of blood raining down on the pavement. Our grunts drowned out all other sounds, although I could vaguely hear shouting, and it occurred to me that I'd left Levi unprotected, that Michael could attack while I was busy with Gabriel. The thought cost me. Distracted, Gabriel got the upper hand—or, rather, foot, bringing it down with all his might on my forearm. The snap of bone was loud, and my bellow even louder. Scrambling to my feet, I cradled my broken arm against my body, making sure the bones were aligned before I started to heal.

"That was a shit move," I accused.

Gabriel tossed his head back and laughed, his delight in my pain more than evident. Time to end this. Spreading my wings, I allowed my flames to burn higher and brighter than ever before. They danced and swirled around me in a firestorm. A look of concern flashed across Gabriel's face. I saw him glance over my shoulder before bringing his attention back to me. *Yeah. You should be worried, dickwad. You piss off Lucifer; you pay the price.*

With a flick of a wing, I sent a fireball his way. He dodged with a startled "Hey!" but wasn't fast enough for the second one. Or third. Within seconds, he was ablaze, running in circles with his arms and wings flapping, screaming louder than any girl.

I let him suffer for a little longer before calling my fire back, and Gabriel was left curled on the ground, unscathed but sobbing. I rolled him onto his back with my foot and, resting my heel on his chest, stared down into his face.

"You think you're better than me? You think you're stronger than me? Think again. You'd do better to work with me than against me."

Turning my back on him, I looked at the others, standing there with their mouths open. Dacian had Michael in a chokehold, and Levi looked ready to self-combust.

"Shall we go to the archives?" Brushing dust from my pants, I smiled brightly, threaded my fingers with Levi's, and headed toward the street, where a new hover vehicle had arrived. "Let him go, Dacian," I commanded without glancing back.

"The sword…" Michael sputtered.

I looked back over my shoulder to where my brother was rubbing his neck and watching Dacian warily as he followed me.

"All in good time," I said.

I'd always been the one to play by the rules, always done as I was told. They didn't have to know that Dacian already had the sword in his possession. It was his call whether he returned it to my brothers or not, but I couldn't help feeling relieved when he hadn't. We needed to find God and then rescue him, and for that, two swords were better than one.

The three of us piled into the backseat of the hovercar, and I directed it to the plantation house. As we glided away, I watched through the window as Michael helped Gabriel to his feet, the shaken look on both their faces reward enough after everything they'd put me through. And then the guilt kicked in. I'd used my flames to hurt someone. Okay, the hurt had been temporary, but still. I'd used it.

Levi squeezed my knee. "You did what you had to do."

I placed my hand over his. "I know." As much as

I regretted my actions, I also knew that if I had to, I'd do it again.

As we traveled through Heaven, Levi gazed out the window with interest. Even though some parts of Heaven were in disrepair, other parts were still pristine and beautiful.

"I never imagined Heaven would be like this," Levi said in wonder as we drove past a building that was half-collapsed, the roof and one wall gone to rubble. Rocks, debris, and rubbish littered the area, and everything was an unattractive, orange-tinged brown color.

"It's not meant to be like this," I replied.

"You notice it's a different color than before?" Dacian asked me.

I nodded. Yes, the last time Heaven had faltered, the invading color had been grey. We now knew grey was the color of evil. This time we had brown. Was that the color of sickness? Death? I pondered this as we drove further out, past the Garden of Eden, which was thankfully still in its pristine state, and then through rain forests, waterfalls, and wilderness.

"The archives are out here?" Levi asked his voice reflecting his surprise.

"Yup, in God's original home."

We glided to a stop in front of an old plantation-style house, painted white with columns supporting the roof. The jungle surrounding it had crept forward, and vines snaked up the side of the house. While the house wasn't in complete disrepair like almost every other part of Heaven, there was a faint air of neglect about it.

"Wow," Levi whispered.

I grinned. This was probably overwhelming to a human. Even when a mortal soul left its earthly body and ascended to Heaven, they never got to see this place. No one but God's family knew of its existence, and with good reason. All of God's plans were here—the blueprints of the realms he'd created, all his creatures big and small. His future plans.

I led the way up the path to the massive door. Before I'd even touched the handle, the door swung open silently, allowing us entry.

Stepping inside was like stepping back to my childhood. This was where my brothers and I had grown up. We'd been born here, had grown into young adults in this house before moving to Heaven Central and taking up our roles.

The floorboards creaked beneath us—another familiar sound. Michael had often grumbled to our father about fixing them, but Dad always chuckled and said he liked the noise. It stopped Michael and Gabriel from sneaking up on him.

"This is...amazing." Levi and Dacian were both gazing around at the high ceilings covered in murals, the decadent artwork on the walls, the luxurious rugs spread over the floor. The house was a mishmash of styles, most of the items gifts from other deities, Dad's own creations, and others looking to win favor.

"Where are the scrolls?" Dacian asked, swinging his gaze back to me.

"In the study." I led the way through the living room and dining room, then into the study, which was the size of Levi's entire apartment. I stopped just inside the doorway and inhaled. I could still smell Dad here. Closing my eyes, I pictured him sitting behind his desk, lifting his head when he heard me scamper through the door, a warm smile welcoming me, even though I knew I was interrupting his work.

"What are you working on, Papa?" Always curious, I skipped across the floor, my bare feet making no sound. Rounding the corner of the desk, I squealed in delight when he scooped me up and onto his knee.

"A new home, Lucy-loo. See here?" He pointed to the parchment spread out on the desk before him.

My tiny fingers traced over the drawings there. "For us?"

"Yes." He nodded, rubbing a big hand up and down my back. Settling against his side, I tried to hold back the yawn that threatened.

"Mama too?" I asked hopefully.

The silence stretched before he cleared his throat and answered, "Perhaps. If that is what she wishes."

"Why doesn't she want to live with us, Papa? Doesn't she love us anymore?"

"Oh, my darling Lucifer, never think that your mother doesn't love you. Together, we created you. You are the essence of us both, and you'll always have a connection with her. But she's from a different world, my child, one that was not so understanding of our union."

"I'm sorry I made you sad, Papa." Tears filled my eyes, and my voice wobbled.

He wrapped me tightly in his arms, giving me the kind of big bear hug only a father can give. "You haven't made me sad, pumpkin. Your mother will visit soon, I promise."

I had been six years old, and I never saw my mother again. God didn't make empty promises, so I knew he'd tried, probably desperately, to convince her to return. Through a child's eyes, I'd watched the heartache and hurt he struggled to hide from us. I barely remembered my mother. She'd left when I was four, and after that last conversation with my father in this study, I'd never asked after her again.

"Everything okay?" Levi's hand on my shoulder made me jump.

"Yeah, just...memories." And a lonely pang that made me realize how much I missed not only my father but my family. Even the mother I barely remembered.

"So, what are we looking for, exactly?" Dacian asked, running his fingers over the scrolls stacked atop each other on the bookshelves.

"I'm not sure, to be honest. Anything that he may have been working on after Hell? He disappeared after creating it, so maybe he moved on to another dimension?"

"Did he ever talk about anything like that?"

"No, but I was all caught up in the excitement of my promotion. I wasn't paying attention to anything else he may have planned." I sat in the chair behind the desk, closing my eyes for a brief moment to hold off the wave of memories that threatened to bombard me. We'd spent a lot of time here in his study, me sitting on his lap and helping him with his plans. I grinned at my own naiveté. I'd probably been a major pain in his ass, but he always welcomed my interruptions.

Forcing myself to focus on the present rather than the past, I studied the desk. Several scraps of parchment were spread across the top. I rifled through them, looking for anything that might give us a clue about his location. At the bottom of the pile, I found a blueprint of Hell. I lifted it to the top, studying it intently. I could see beyond the borders that he'd left a pocket realm for expansion if I needed it. I flipped the parchment over, confirming there was nothing on the back.

"Hey! This one is about the swords." Levi hurried over and spread the scroll he had in his hands across the desk. On it was two swords, one with a blue glow, the other with red flames.

"So it is." I leaned closer to read my father's handwriting. The Sword of Angels and the Sword of Souls. Both powerful weapons that only the ruler of their respective realms could wield. "See? Here." I pointed to the words. "Only the ruler of the realm can use the sword."

"So?" Levi asked.

"So how come both you and Dacian were able to use the Sword of Angels? And what about the zombie ghosts on Earth? You also touched my sword with no ill effects. That isn't how they were designed."

"Can I try something?" Dacian asked.

I glanced at him quizzically. "What?"

"Let me see if I can touch your sword."

"Why?"

"As an experiment. Perhaps we can work out whether your father's invention failed somewhere. I mean, yes, they are powerful weapons, but what if something went a little haywire and they can, in fact, be wielded by anyone?"

It wouldn't help us find my father, but I could see the benefit of knowing the truth. It would also tell me if my brothers could steal the sword from me. Maybe that had been their intention all along—tell me how to create the Sword of Souls, then take it for themselves.

"Let's do it." I withdrew the sword from between my wings and held it across my outstretched palms. "Take it," I told Dacian.

Stepping up to the sword, he gave his hands a shake, then wrapped his fingers around the handle. The sizzle of flesh was instant and unmistakable. "Ow. Fuck!" Quickly releasing the sword, Dacian backed away, blowing on his burnt hand.

"Are you okay? Do you need me to heal you?" I offered.

"I'm good. All healed." He held his palm up, showing us that the burn was gone entirely.

"Let me try," Levi said. Before I could stop him, he'd picked up the sword. And absolutely nothing happened.

Dacian and I looked at each other. What the hell was going on?

"How come you can hold it?" Dacian demanded.

Levi shrugged, a grin curving his lips. He started to wave the sword through the air, making the flames dance until I snatched it from him and tucked it back between my wings.

"Dacian, check the scroll, will you?" I said. "Look for any clue that can tell us how this is possible."

"On it."

We spent the next few hours scouring the study, going through scroll after scroll, searching for any kind of hint as to Dad's whereabouts. I found a scroll about my mother that gave me pause. Did I want to know more about the woman who had given birth to me and then left? Dad had never said a bad word about her, and I knew, based on all the times I'd caught him with a sad look on his face, that he missed her. Possibly loved her; otherwise, why would they have had children together? I slid the scroll under my wing, tucking it safely away. I'd read it later when all of this was over, and things were back to normal.

"Nothing. I've got nothing." Dacian cursed, flopping back in his chair and running his fingers through his hair. "This is a bust."

"I have to agree," I replied. We'd found no indication that Dad had another project on the go, no secret realms, no hidden places. The scroll about the swords had revealed nothing about why Levi had been able to hold it.

"What next?" Levi asked.

I shrugged. "I don't know about you, but I'm beat."

"So, we go back to Earth?"

He sounded disappointed, but I was already shaking my head. "No. We'll go back to my apartment here. There's still work to be done in Heaven. The answer wasn't in the scrolls like I'd hoped, but I'm not convinced it isn't here."

"You want to examine the decaying buildings," Dacian guessed, and I nodded.

"If we can pinpoint where it started, maybe that will give us a clue."

"It worked last time," Dacian agreed.

Last time, evil souls had tried to corrupt Heaven. While they had wreaked havoc and disruption for a short period, we'd gotten things under control relatively quickly. This time, I felt like I was on the back foot. I didn't have all the facts. I wasn't sure how long Heaven had been in this state, or precisely when it had started, or what the other symptoms were.

My brothers had a lot to answer for, allowing things to get this bad.

EIGHT

My apartment was exactly as I'd left it over a millennia ago, a townhouse on the small side that I adored. A cleaning service came in weekly to keep it pristine, and word of my return had spread, so the kitchen had been fully stocked, toiletries neatly placed in the bathroom, and fresh robes hung in my wardrobe. Dacian had returned to his own place, and I hoped my brothers would leave him alone. Just in case they didn't, I'd given him a quick lesson on how to construct a mental shield to keep them out of his head. I had a horrible suspicion he wasn't safe, and it ate at me that one of God's own guards was at risk in Heaven.

"You worry too much." Levi slipped his arms

around my waist and pulled me back against his chest.

"There's a lot to worry about."

"Why don't I take your mind off it?"

He nuzzled at my neck, and I sighed, arching to give him better access. "I think that sounds like a great idea."

"Let's take a shower," he said, shuffling us across the floor backward toward the bathroom.

I laughed. "What is it with you and sex in the bathroom?"

"Hey, can I help it if I love you naked and wet?" He spun me to face him, pulling me close and kissing me, the force and passion behind his embrace overwhelming in its intensity. Knees weak, I pressed against him, twining my arms around his neck.

As he pushed me up against the shower wall, Levi's hands tugged at my clothes, but it was taking too long. I was impatient for his touch. With a whisper of magic, I undressed us both, and our clothes dropped to the floor.

"Neat trick," he said, chuckling, before plastering himself against me, skin to skin. Thank the Lord he'd pinned me to the tile, holding me up because all the strength had left my legs. I was a boneless mass of sensation.

His mouth crushed my lips as our tongues danced a duet, and his hands flamed my skin as they explored every inch of my body. I had never experienced anything like this with any lover ever before, and I felt like I'd never be able to get enough of him.

Levi continued his exquisite torture, licking and nibbling until I felt my whole body was going to combust right there in the shower. Dragging his face up to mine, I could see the lust and desire in his eyes and the way they lit up as he saw the same reflected in my eyes. As his mouth again plundered mine, I surrendered myself to him totally.

Coming down from my high, I noticed something I hadn't before. "What's this?" I asked.

Levi had turned his face into the spray of water, and I was studying his lean, muscled back, admiring the rivulets of water as they cascaded over his shoulders and down to his tight as steel ass. But what had caught my attention was a black mark on the back of his right shoulder. It looked like a stamp or brand that had gotten wet, and the ink had smudged, making it hard to decipher the design.

"What's what?" He didn't turn, busy shampooing his hair. The bubbles distorted the mark until I jerked him out from under the spray to get a better look.

"Is this a tattoo? Have you always had it?"

"What? Nah, I don't have any tattoos." He laughed. "It's probably dirt!"

I rubbed at the mark, but it didn't budge. Not dirt.

"You still feel hot, you know," I commented, placing my palm over the mark and feeling the warmth of his flesh.

He shrugged. "Told you, I feel fine. Maybe I just run hotter these days?"

"Do you think passing through into another dimension could have changed you?"

"Will you just let it go?" The edge to his voice caught me by surprise, and when he jerked away from my touch and stepped out of the shower, I realized I'd pushed too far. But was I wrong? Levi's body temperature was definitely above normal—for a human.

"I feel fine. I *am* fine! The only thing wrong is you nagging me."

Wrapping a towel around his hips, he flung open the bathroom door, leaving me standing, dazed, in the shower. We'd gone from hot and heavy to frigid within two seconds, and my head was reeling. His mood swings not only gave me whiplash, but it just wasn't like him at all. He was the calmest, even-tempered person I'd ever met, yet...

Was I overreacting? He'd been through a traumatic experience. Lashing out could be in response to that.

Finishing up in the shower, I quickly dried and dressed, meeting Levi in the living room.

"I'm sorry." I didn't quite know what I was apologizing for, only that it seemed to be the right thing to do. My worry had angered him, and for that, I was sorry. But I wasn't sorry for worrying.

"It's okay." Pulling me into a hug, he gave me a tight squeeze. "I'm sorry, too."

We were interrupted by a knock at the door and Dacian's voice demanding we get our lazy asses out of bed. Flinging open the door, I scowled at him.

"We're up, thank you very much."

"Good. I've got a plan." He strode in and stood with hands-on-hips in the middle of the room.

"Oh?" It was nice to have a plan. I liked plans.

Only lately, it felt like I'd been terrible at coming up with a good one.

"I'm going to get a team of Seraph angels together, and we're going to search Heaven from top to bottom."

"Okay." It wasn't a brilliant plan, but it was something.

"You have a better idea?" Dacian challenged.

"I thought I'd go to HQ and search Dad's office."

"You don't think your brothers have done that already?"

I shrugged. "Even if they have, I doubt they'd tell me. They say they want him found, but I don't see them doing much searching."

"Exactly. I don't want them to know what I'm doing, so I'm going to say we're documenting the damage and making a list of repairs. Heaven may be deteriorating, but no one is attempting to repair anything. I can turn that around."

I thought about it for a moment. Dacian was right. Heaven would be in better shape if someone at least attempted to fix it. And while he was doing that, he could also look for clues about God. Brilliant plan. I told him so and winced a little at the overly bright smile he gave me. Dacian probably didn't receive much praise from my brothers, and once again, my anger started to bubble to the surface.

"Let's split up," I said. "Levi and I will go to HQ. You go gather your team and start your search. Meet back here later?"

***

DAD'S OFFICE was exactly as I remembered it—massive and made of glass with sleek surfaces. The opposite of the plantation house in the jungle. I'd just settled into his chair when the door slid open, and Michael walked in, body stiff and face passive. But his eyes—oh, his eyes were spitting fire.

"What are you doing?" His voice was level but laced with annoyance. Maybe even anger. Michael always liked to be in control of his emotions and rarely displayed his feelings one way or the other. But I was convinced that he was pulling strings behind the scenes and watching his little games play out underneath it all.

"I'm searching for clues about Dad." Ignoring him, I began swiping through the electronic device on the desk. It was fully charged. Interesting.

"We've already done that."

"What did you find?"

"Nothing." It was the split-second hesitation before he answered that gave him away. *Liar.*

"Can't hurt to take another look, then." The electronic device yielded nothing, but I suspected it wouldn't. My brothers had wiped it. I needed a physical clue. Something small, something insignificant that they would have overlooked.

"Why don't you want him found?" I asked conversationally, rifling through drawers.

"I do want him found."

I couldn't contain my snort of disbelief.

"No, seriously. I do. It's just..." He glanced over his shoulder at the closed door, then looked back at me.

"What?" I stopped, looking at him.

"Don't tell him I said anything, but —" He broke off, face twisting in a grimace.

"Who?"

"Gabriel. I think he may have done something."

"To Dad?"

Michael nodded, looking down at his feet. "I need your help, Lucy."

I sat back, eyes round with disbelief. Over by the bookcase, Levi had frozen with a book open in his hand, watching us both.

"Explain," I said.

"I'm ashamed to say we've known Dad was missing since day one. But...you weren't here to kick up a fuss, and we honestly thought he was visiting with you for a bit and then having a vacation. We were just caught up, I suppose, in the ego boost of having Heaven to ourselves that we didn't notice he'd been gone so long, and without a word. And then we thought...perhaps he'd died. But we knew Heaven would panic if word got out, so we kept it quiet."

"Only now Heaven itself is outing your secret."

He nodded. "And when I think back, it was Gabriel who suggested not saying anything. It was Gabriel who struck a deal with the Xoelaxians for the time device on Earth. It's Gabriel who wants to rule it all."

"So you're saying everything is Gabriel's fault? And what? You just went along for the ride? Didn't have the balls to speak up or stop him?"

"I was—still am—afraid of him." He met my eyes, and the pleading in them was real.

I looked across at Levi, who arched a brow. Did I believe my brother or not? He was laying all the blame at Gabriel's feet. While I could see that our brother was the ringleader in all of this, I couldn't accept that Michael was a victim, that he'd been bullied into going along with Gabriel's plans. Something more was going on here.

With a slight nod of my head, I smiled at him. "Thank you for being honest with me, Michael. It means a lot."

"You believe me?" He sounded surprised.

Of course not, you idiot, I thought, but out loud, I said, "There's no reason not to. Is there?"

"No. I'm telling the truth, I swear."

"Your word is all I need. Do you have any theories about where Dad could be?"

He shook his head. "No. Sorry. I've looked in all the places I know he likes to visit, but there's been no sign of him. I wish I could be of more help."

"Actually, there is something you could do to help."

"Oh?"

I nodded. "Keep Gabriel away. I don't want another confrontation like yesterday. It's best he doesn't know what we're doing, and if he sees me here, I'm afraid he'll have another tantrum."

"I'll keep him away. I promise." Michael's smile lit up his face, and I smiled in return, raising my hand in farewell when he spun and left the office, the door sliding closed behind him.

Several seconds passed in silence before Levi said, "Do you believe him?"

"Not at all."

"Good. Because I just found this." Levi held up a scrap of paper.

"What is it?"

"A note." He held it out to me. "Found it in this book about the seals."

I recognized my father's handwriting but couldn't quite make out the words. "What does it say?"

"Shadow Falls," Levi replied.

"Weird."

"Coincidence? I think not."

"You think they planted it?" I wouldn't put it past them, plus Levi had found it rather quickly.

He shrugged. "Possibly. But it's a lead, so we should check it out. There are a bunch of tunnels and caves beneath Shadow Falls. He could be down there, possibly incapacitated in some way. And it's the location Gabriel chose for the orb. There has to be some significance in that."

CHAPTER

NINE

After leaving a message for Dacian, Levi and I returned to Shadow Falls. Strolling down Main Street, nodding hello to all the townsfolk we passed, Levi muttered, "This is so fucking weird."

"What is?" I was watching the woman across the street. She looked to be in her fifties and walked a little white fluffball of a dog on a leash.

"That no time has passed here. I was in the Xoelax dimension for weeks, then we went to Heaven for a day or so, and now we're back here, and it's just weird. Exactly how much time has passed since I closed the shop?"

"Don't quote me, but a couple of hours, maybe more?" I shrugged, eyes intent on the woman. Her dog stopped to pee, and a flash of irritation crossed her face. She jerked on the leash, not letting the dog stop and take care of business. "Excuse me one second." Before Levi could reply, I crossed the street and approaching the woman.

"You need to stop and let your dog pee." I didn't bother with niceties, for I already knew what I needed to know. She abused this poor animal. Kicked it. Starved it. My blood boiled.

"How I treat my dog is none of your business. Go away." She shooed me with a wave of her hand and went to move past me, but I stepped sideways, blocking her. The dog whined, and I looked down at him. His big brown eyes looked soulfully back at me, melting my heart.

"Oh, it is very much my business," I said, squatting to give her dog a pat. "I'm Lucifer, CEO of Hell, and I have a spot reserved for people like you."

"Oh. You're one of them." Her snooty tone grated on my nerves, and I rose to my feet, stepping closer so she could see the fire I unleashed in my eyes.

"I kid you not," I spoke softly, with menace. "I'm not off my meds, and I'm not a mental patient or any of the excuses people like you throw around. I am the Devil, and I will make you suffer as you make this creature suffer."

She paled, a trembling hand clutching her throat. "But—you can't be."

"I assure you I very much am. I want you to re-home this animal immediately to a loving family who will treat it right. You have no capacity, not until you deal with your own demons. Until that time, no pets."

The little dog yapped. "It's okay, sweetheart, we'll get you sorted," I said to him, then turned my attention back to his owner. "Are we clear?"

"Yes." She nodded her head so fast I feared it might topple off.

"You'll find a new home for this dog?" I pressed.

"Yes. I think my sister and her family would be delighted to have him."

"Make it happen. Repent your sins, make amends, and maybe—*just maybe*—I won't see you in Hell. Not everyone gets this chance. Don't blow it."

"I won't." Scooping the dog into her arms, she hurried away.

"You continue to amaze me." Levi smiled, draping his arm around my shoulders when I returned to his side, and we continued on our way to the town square.

"Oh? Why's that?"

"Because even though everyone on this planet

believes you're evil, you still want to help them. You could have let that slide, but you didn't. You're trying to save souls."

"Of course. I don't *want* to see them in Hell. It makes me sad that there's so much work to be done here. There's a design flaw in humans that makes them this way."

"I wouldn't say design flaw. That would mean it affects everyone. Maybe a glitch? An anomaly that only affects some but not others?" Levi suggested.

"Perhaps. Still too many. Why would you want to hurt your fellow man? Or defenseless creatures? It's beyond imagination...and makes me so damn mad."

"I think this is why God chose you."

I glanced at him. "Oh?'

"To run Hell. Because you're passionate about it, about keeping souls on the right path. From what I've seen, your brothers don't give a damn about humans. But you care, and it shows."

"We won't know until we find him." I shrugged off his compliments, but my heart was ready to burst with happiness. Levi understood me. My brothers never had, and, I suspected, never would. They were still trying to work out my angle when the truth was, I didn't have one.

"Are we going in the same way?" We'd come to a stop at the town square and the massive sinkhole with yellow police tape around it.

"Yep." I waited until a group of people had passed us, then grabbed hold of Levi and whisked us into the sinkhole, flying until we reached the bottom. Using my magic, I summoned a ball of light and held it in my palm.

"Where do we even start?" Levi kicked at the rubble underfoot.

This part of the labyrinth had collapsed the last time we were here. Although I hadn't searched every last tunnel and cave, I also hadn't come across any indication that dad was here. But that was generally the case when someone went missing, wasn't it? They either didn't want to be found, or someone else didn't want them to be found. I had to face the facts. There wasn't going to be a big neon sign pointing the way.

"Do you think you'd sense him if you got near him?" I asked.

Levi had made a connection of sorts through the Sword of Souls. Maybe it would be of use during our search.

"Doubtful. It's never worked that way before, but who knows." He shrugged, stepping past me and into a dark passageway. I followed, sending the ball of light ahead of us to guide the way.

Our search of the tunnels was long, arduous, and unsuccessful. We found no signs of Dad, no hidden chambers, and to say I was disheartened was an understatement. We were in the massive cave where the orb from Xoelax had been hidden when a group of ten or more revenants suddenly appeared, and they were coming for us.

"Shit!" I scrambled, rushing to put myself between Levi and the revenants, some of whom were carrying weapons. As they approached, I could see them scooping up rocks. These guys meant business.

"Who are they?" Levi stood with his legs apart, knees bent, ready for battle.

"Revenants. They've been in limbo for too long, and now their souls have left them, sending their bodies back to Earth. They're just shells."

"Angry shells, by the looks of things."

He wasn't wrong. Readying myself with the Sword of Souls, I braced myself for their attack. When it came, it was brutal. The three revenants leading the charge pulled out guns from behind their backs and opened fire. Holy shit balls, that was unexpected! Spreading my wings, I did my best to shield Levi, wincing as a hail of bullets tore through them.

"Stay behind me!" I shouted, slashing and stabbing with the sword, trying to keep them from surrounding us.

"I don't need you to protect me." Levi cursed, and I could hear him moving behind me.

"Don't be stupid! They've got guns, Levi. A bullet will kill you." Why did men have to be so stubborn? Why couldn't he simply do as I asked and stay out of trouble?

Then he moved into view, and I understood why. He was incorporeal. Transparent. A ghost? Had they killed him, and I hadn't noticed? How could that be?

"Relax. I'm fine. Definitely not dead." He chuckled, then threw a firebolt. With his hands. Just what the fuck was going on here?

A bullet ripping through my shoulder jolted me back to attention. "Okay, assholes, that's quite enough of that, thank you very much!"

Side by side, Levi and I took the revenants down. Their bullets sailed straight through him, as did the rocks, sticks, and various other weapons they used against him. I sustained a few cuts and bruises, but nothing that wouldn't heal. They just stung like the devil—pun intended.

Within minutes, they were dispatched, their glowing red eyes snuffed out, the putrid scent of their scorched flesh hung in the air. I covered my nose with my arm.

"What next?" Levi asked.

"We wait."

"For what?" As he asked, the ground beneath the fallen revenants opened up and sucked their bodies down into the earth. Within seconds, they were gone. The only sign of the battle was the pools of black blood on the ground.

"What happens to them now?" Levi asked.

"Nothing. They're gone. Their souls have already died." I allowed myself to feel the grief of that for a moment until more pressing things became apparent. Turning on him, I demanded, "What in the hell is *this* all about?" I waved my hand up and down, indicating his incorporeal state.

He became corporeal before my eyes, and I couldn't stop myself from poking him in the shoulder just to be sure. He chuckled, and I slapped his arm. "It's not funny! I thought they'd killed you!"

"Nah. Not dead." He performed a neat pirouette, and I wanted to slap him again.

"Explain to me, exactly, what just happened."

He shrugged. "Honestly? I don't really know."

I peered at him intently before blowing out a sigh. Something had changed within Levi at an intrinsic level. Either something had happened to him in the Xoelax realm, or the mere act of being in the realm had altered him. Or maybe that, coupled with going to Heaven, had caused some sort of chain reaction.

"Stop frowning." He gently smoothed out the crease between my brows and then cupped my face. "I'm fine. I feel okay, I promise."

"Levi," I began, "it's not normal for humans to be able to do that."

He chuckled, resting his forehead against mine. "I think we both know I'm no longer human, right? Because you're spot on, humans can't do that. Not even psychics."

"This is my fault." I wanted to cry. I'd never meant him any harm, but I'd dragged him into this whole sorry mess and now look at him. Human one minute, a ghost the next!

"You're assuming it's a bad thing. I think it's more of an...upgrade. I mean, did you see what I could do? Shooting fire from my fingers? Who wouldn't love to be able to do that?" The excitement in his voice was unmistakable, but I wasn't so easily swayed.

"I'm not so sure it's a good thing, either."

"Well, we can stand around here discussing the pros and cons of it, or we can go find your dad. Because either way, we don't know what caused this. We don't know if it's reversible, and I'm not sure I want to reverse it." Entwining his fingers with mine, he looked intently into my eyes for a moment before dazzling me with his smile. "Shall we go?"

"I guess. Dad's not here. But there's something about this place, this cave, that's a magnet for the undead."

"It could have been you they were drawn to. As soulless creatures, doesn't that mean they're evil? They have no conscience, no remorse, and they came after us with weapons. They weren't messing around."

"Why attack me, though? To what end?"

"Maybe they want to break into Hell? Free the evil souls there?" He was only guessing, but I was worried his guesses might be closer to the truth than either of us realized. If the revenants gained access to the millions of souls in Hell, they'd have one heck of an army. I shivered at the thought.

Then my tummy rumbled.

"Let's go to the diner. I'm hungry."

Walking into the diner was like coming home. It was comfortable and familiar, and with everything that had been going on recently, I was grateful for it. Sliding into what I considered our booth, I flashed a smile at Sophie, the waitress who used to spit in people's food if they didn't tip. Thankfully, she'd mended her ways—due to _my_ intervention, of course. I signaled her over.

Levi chuckled. "You don't want to look at the menu first?"

"I bet you already know what you want."

The clanging of the door opening caught my attention. I looked over Levi's shoulder, a smile splitting my face when Detective Jared Morrison walked in, his partner Detective Nicole James—Nic for short—close on his heels. I waved.

"Hi, guys. Wanna join us?" I offered.

"Sure." Jared slid in next to me, and Nic took the seat next to Levi.

"How's business?" I asked once we were all settled. Now that we'd sent the soul stealer who'd been wreaking havoc in Shadow Falls back to his own dimension, I was hoping the two detectives were enjoying a slower pace. I was also thrilled to see the loving glances they exchanged. I was a sucker for a happy ending.

"Thankfully, nothing unusual to report," Jared told me, picking up the menu to peruse the offerings.

Nic shrugged. "Just the usual drug dealers and domestic violence. Same shit, different day."

It saddened me that humans were so self-destructive. I was sure father hadn't envisioned any of this for his creations but left to their own devices, and despite the sense of right and wrong he'd hard-wired into them, some still chose the wrong path. It was fascinating and appalling at the same time.

Sophie arrived, pad and pen in hand. "Y'all ready to order?" She briefly met my eyes, and her lips twitched in what I suppose was meant to resemble a smile. Then she returned her attention to her pad, refusing to look at any of us.

"Burger and fries for me, please, and a chocolate shake," I said.

"A chocolate shake?" Levi asked in surprise. "Since when do you even know what a chocolate shake is?"

"I have been here before, you know."

"Here, as in this diner? Or…."

"On Earth. Where do you think I get my coffee beans from? They won't grow in Hell. I've tried."

"Oh," Nic squeaked.

I looked across at her. "What?"

"I've never thought of you just popping in to visit before."

I shrugged. "Earth is nice. I like it here." Glancing at Sophie, who was looking more and more uncomfortable, I prompted the others, "Sophie's waiting for your orders, guys. We can chat after."

I don't know why I thought I'd get to enjoy a meal in peace for a change, but I'd just bitten into my burger—which had arrived remarkably fast—when I felt the evil in the room. Chewing slowly, I surveyed the customers in the diner. It didn't take me long to spot him. Sitting by himself, a newspaper spread out before him, was a middle-aged man, balding and squeezed into a suit a size too small.

"What's up?" Levi nudged me, drawing my attention.

"Just another sorry soul on the wrong path," I muttered, keeping an eye on the man as I continued my meal. I didn't have to intervene, of course. I could let it slide and deal with him in Hell, but I was happier if I could save souls before they came my way. So when the man got up to leave, I quickly excused myself and followed him out.

"Excuse me." I caught up with him in the parking lot, caught the flash of his surprise on his face, which quickly gave way to irritation.

"What is it?" he snapped, glancing at his watch.

"I wanted you to know I know. And if you don't cut it out, your soul is going to Hell."

His eyebrows shot up into what was left of his hairline, and he tugged at his tie. "What are you even talking about?"

"You know."

"Look, honey," he said, his tone patronizing, "I think you may have skipped your meds today. Run along and bother someone else. I'm not interested."

I blew out a breath. The ones on the wrong path were all the same. They always needed convincing.

Blinking, I let the hellfire glow in my eyes and leaned in close, so he got a good look.

"I'm Lucifer. Lucy to my friends. And I know you've been embezzling from your employer. First of all, you need to stop that shit right now. And second of all, you need to make amends. Fix it. Repent. And then, maybe, I won't see you in Hell."

His mouth dropped open, and I almost laughed. Schooling my face, I said sternly, "Unless, of course, you like the idea of burning in the pit for all of eternity? In which case, stay on this path."

I practically heard his heart rate accelerate. His face went pale and sweat beaded on his forehead.

"Hell is...real?" he stammered.

"Of course. Do you want to visit?"

"No." It was barely a whisper, but it was all I needed.

"Then get your shit together, Kevin. I mean, yes, there are worse crimes than yours, but what you're doing is wrong. You and I both know it."

"What do I do?" he cried, wringing his hands.

"Tell your employer. Payback the money. Take whatever punishment comes your way. Live a better life."

"But..." He looked around furtively, then back at

me. "I was desperate! I needed the money for my mother's cancer treatment."

I nodded. "I know, but it was wrong to steal it. And come on now, you've taken three times as much as you needed. Greed isn't an attractive trait in a man, Kevin."

"I'm sorry," he all but sobbed.

I patted his shoulder. "Fix it, or I'll see you in Hell. Understood?"

"Understood."

I beamed at him. "Fantastic. Great to meet you, Kevin. Have a nice day."

I bounced back into the diner, pleased I'd saved another soul today. It made up, only slightly, for the revenants we'd destroyed. The thought sobered me, and my smile vanished. We had to find Dad and get the Pearly Gates open, pronto.

ELEVEN

"You're frowning again." Levi's words pulled me from my pondering. Jared and Nic had left after receiving a call about a case they were working on. I helped myself to the fries on Nic's plate.

"None of this makes sense," I muttered.

"What?"

"How can you become incorporeal and shoot fire from your hands? How does that work? What happened to you?" I turned to look at him, studying him intently. He was still hot, his body radiating an unnatural warmth.

"Oh, we're back to that again?" He picked up his coffee and took a gulp.

"It's not something I can ignore, Levi."

"I haven't done anything wrong."

"I didn't say you had!" I protested.

"Then why can't you let it drop? I've changed. I don't know why, and nor do you. Why can't you just accept that it is what it is and not over-analyze every little thing?"

His words stung. "I don't want to fight with you, Levi. I just want to understand what's happened."

"So you can change me back?" he challenged.

Even if I had the capacity, I wasn't sure I'd do it. Not against his wishes. But we didn't know exactly what he was capable of or what the consequences would be.

"I just want you to be safe. We don't know what this is. Are you going to change further? What if you stop being you?" I tried to dial back the emotion, but it leaked through. I knew he felt it by the way he cocked his head and considered me.

"You're concerned," he said.

"Of course."

"What do you suggest?" Maybe he was prepared to meet me halfway after all.

Leaning in, I cupped his face in my hands and kissed him hard. "I love you," I whispered against his lips.

I felt him smile. His hand slipped around the nape of my neck and squeezed. "I love you, too, crazy woman."

"Hey!" I laughed, moving out of his embrace. "Watch who you're calling crazy. I could singe your ass!"

"Pretty sure I could give as good as I can get." He winked, and I couldn't help the snort that escaped. "I have an idea." He sobered and reached for my hand, entwining his fingers with mine.

"Oh?"

"What's happening with me has to do with heat and fire, yes?"

"Yes. And becoming incorporeal," I added.

"That too. So maybe the answer is in Hell."

He had a point. Hell was the epitome of heat and fire, but I wasn't sure taking him there was a good idea. If jumping dimensions caused this, what would visiting Hell do to him?

"Stop worrying." It was like he could read my mind. "What's done is done. How much worse could it get?"

I gasped. "Oh, don't say that! Never say that. Famous last words and all that shit."

"Look, I've been to the Xoelax dimension, survived being hunted by the Xoelaxian people, and

I've gone to Heaven! Take me to Hell. I want to see where you live." His grin and the way he rubbed his thumb against my palm had me distracted.

"Okay. What's the worst that could happen?" Giving in, I wrapped my arms around his neck and moved in close, nuzzling his neck. What harm could it do? He was already changing, and maybe Hell had the answers we needed.

"He's a fire demon." Ashliel circled Levi, assessing him from head to toe. Nodding to herself, she stopped with her hands on her hips and cocked her head at me. "I'm surprised you didn't see it."

"A fire demon? You sure?"

We both stared at Levi, who threw his hands up in the air.

"Whatever, guys. Check out this view. It's amazing!" He didn't seem concerned by this latest turn of events. He was much more interested in the skyline view from my massive windows. He was right—it *was* an amazing view. I'd often stood where he was standing and looked out over my kingdom. Wingless Demons patrolled the streets on foot while their winged counterparts took to the skies.

His lack of concern worried me. I rubbed at my forehead, an ache beginning behind my eyes. His body was changing, his DNA mutating in ways that weren't normal. Not for a human. And here he was, more interested in the view! Men.

"How did this happen?" I asked Ashliel.

"Are you serious?" She snorted out a laugh, and I frowned so hard my eyebrows hurt. "Oh, this is priceless." She continued to chuckle.

"Cut it out, Ash. I'm not in the mood."

"It's what you *were* in the mood for; that's the problem." Again, she chuckled, and I was ready to wipe the grin right off her beautiful face.

"Okay, okay." Relenting, she clasped my hands and sucked in a deep breath. "You did this. You changed him."

"What? I did not!" I snatched my hands away, aghast at her suggestion. I would never harm Levi. Never.

This got his attention, and he turned from the window, arms crossed over his chest, his full attention on Ashliel. "She did?" He didn't seem angry or worried. Just curious.

Ashliel nodded. "Yup. You obviously didn't know you were doing it, Lucy. It just came naturally to you."

"What did I do?" I whispered, horrified that I was responsible for this.

"You bit him."

The room went silent as we digested her words. My mind replayed each and every moment Levi and I had been together. It took a while. Levi beat me to it.

"She did. I remember. It wasn't a bite, just a nip. A love bite."

"Where? Where did I bite you?" I demanded.

"On my shoulder."

"Show me!"

I began tugging at the hem of his t-shirt, pulling it up. Laughing, he pushed my hands away. "Okay, okay, I'll do it. Stop helping."

In one smooth movement, he swept the t-shirt up and over his head. I was momentarily distracted by the expanse of his naked chest and abs. He was more defined. The tan lines faded, revealing a smooth expanse of golden skin. Still delicious, but...I bit my lip and poked him in the shoulder, prompting him to turn so I could see his back.

And there it was. The dark smudge I'd seen on his shoulder while we were showering. It had turned into a fully-formed mark. My mark.

"It's…"

"It's what?" He twisted his head, glancing over his shoulder.

"The key," I squeaked, hand over my mouth.

"What do you mean, the key?" He turned to face me, brow furrowing in concern. "Lucy? What's wrong? What are you talking about?"

"It shouldn't be here! On you! The key is safe, hidden. Complete. There is no fourth piece."

"What on Earth are you talking about?"

But I couldn't answer. I was in shock. This couldn't be. It was impossible. Numbly, I tried to comprehend what I was seeing. The dark smudge I saw in the shower had evolved, but maybe it wasn't finished. Perhaps it was something else, and its resemblance to the key was purely coincidental. I couldn't even begin to cope with the fact that Levi had a growing tattoo on his shoulder in the first place. One I unknowingly put there.

"Come on, Lucy," he cajoled, resting his hands on my shoulders and peering into my eyes. "Spit it out. What is the key?"

"The mark looks very similar to the key. It may be identical. It's the key to the gates of Hell."

"Ah. No wonder you freaked out."

"Why aren't you?"

"Freaked out?" he asked. "Let me see, I was dragged into the Xoelax dimension and spent weeks trying to survive being eaten by the Xoelaxians. Then you rescued me and took me with you to Heaven, then came back to Earth and fought some revenants, and now here we are in Hell. A little mark on my shoulder is nothing to worry about."

"You think?" I sank down onto the sofa in the corner of my office. Across the room, the multi-screen display showed hundreds of images, constantly flickering, giving us a live feed from Earth. I stared at it with blind eyes while my mind tried to accept the fact that Levi had a piece of the key marked on his skin.

"Tell me about the key. You were muttering something about three pieces?" he prompted.

"Unlike Heaven, Hell is kept locked. Not to keep souls out, but to keep them in. People figured out pretty quickly that Hell isn't a great place to be and kept trying to break out, so I built the gates."

"And made a key."

"And made a key, yes. But it was too risky to keep it here. If someone were to steal the key, they could open the gates, and the evil souls would flood Earth. So I hid it on Earth, in the safekeeping of a believer."

"A believer? Like a religious person? A priest?"

I nodded. "Yes. But then word got out that there was a key on Earth, and it was getting harder and harder to keep it hidden, so the priest broke it into three pieces. He gave the other two pieces to different priests for safekeeping."

"Must have been difficult to break a key."

"It isn't a normal key. It's more like a talisman. Anyway, over the years, the three pieces have been passed down for safekeeping, but when two of the keepers died, the pieces of key were buried with them."

"Well, okay, so the pieces are still safe, then."

"Until archeologists dug them up."

Levi's jaw dropped. "Shit! What happened to them?"

"They ended up in a museum."

"Together? In the same museum?"

"Not initially. Which was fine, as long as they were separated and no one figured out the connection."

"But someone did?"

"Eventually. What with technology and the internet, yes, the museums realized they each had a piece of a whole."

"But a piece was still missing?"

"Yes, but it was really more of a shard. And even though the pieces were handed along from priest to priest, there was now a demon on the trail. The demon had conveniently located the two pieces in one location. All he had to do was find the third piece, and he'd have the key to the gates of Hell."

"What happened?"

"He failed. The three pieces changed vessels and are separate once more."

"Changed vessels? What does *that* mean?"

"They were passed on to new keepers. The first time the key was a talisman. This time it's something different. It doesn't matter. What matters is that the design on your shoulder is the same as the design of the key. Or at least very, very, similar."

"So now you think I'm part of the key?" he asked.

"Guys," Ashliel interrupted. I hadn't noticed she'd left the room, but now she came bursting through my office door, a book open in her hands. "I knew I'd seen it somewhere."

"What's that?" I nodded at the book. It looked to be as old as, if not older than, me. I didn't care to talk about my age, but this thing was *ancient*.

"Yeah, it was in the archives. I knew I'd read something about finding your true mate and markings and all that. Here it is." She held the book out to me, and I saw a hand-drawn symbol that resembled the mark on Levi's back.

"It's not the key?" I could see the subtle differences between the two symbols and quickly scanned the text on the page to be sure.

"It's not the key," Ashliel confirmed. "It's the mate's mark. It happens when a supernatural entity, such as yourself—" She indicated me. "—finds their true mate. A mate that destiny, or fate, if you like, has decided is the perfect match for you. So, when you bit Levi, you not only branded him with the mate's mark, but you bound him to you."

"I'm bound?" Levi's voice rose several octaves, and I felt awful for him. Imagine being bound to someone without your knowledge or consent. This was awful. I felt awful.

"I'm so sorry. I didn't realize." What had I done?

"There's more," Ashliel interrupted.

I sighed. This couldn't possibly get any worse. "Let's have it."

"The mark will also change him, at a cellular level, to make him compatible with you. As a species." She closed the book and lifted one shoulder. "I don't think it's that bad, Lucy. Levi doesn't appear to be upset about it. In fact, the energy I'm getting from him is that he likes his new status."

"But I bound him to me. Without his consent! That's a sin."

"You need to take that up with Fate. She set all of this up. Plus, it wouldn't have worked if he wasn't willing."

"Fate? Fate is a person?" Levi asked.

"Sure. She's one of the gods, has her own galaxy, runs it with her sister Destiny."

"Mind. Blown." Turning his attention back to me, Levi cupped my face in his hands. "Ashliel is right. This isn't all that bad. I don't mind being a fire demon. I like how I feel. And being bound to you? Well...I don't think I mind that, either." He slid a hand around the nape of my neck and angled my head back, his hips pressing into mine. "I don't mind it at all."

"Oh," was my well-thought-out answer. With his lips a whisper from mine, my brain had simply stopped functioning. And that musky, chocolatey, whiskey smell of his successfully took my mind off worrying that I'd marked him to wondering how quickly I could get his pants off.

Ashliel coughed, and we both turned our heads, cheek to cheek, to look at her.

"If it makes you feel better, he can also mark you. Now that he's a demon, it's possible. Just return the favor, Levi, and you're good to go. And speaking of going, I'm outta here before I have to bleach my eyeballs."

"Now, there's an idea." The deep rumble of his voice vibrated through me, setting my nerve endings on fire.

"What's that?" I couldn't focus, couldn't think. I could only feel. And the sensation of him pressed against me was all I needed. *He* was all I needed.

"I want to." His lips trailed across my cheek, from my ear to the corner of my lips.

"What?" I had no idea what he was talking about.

"Mark you. Make you mine. If there's one thing that makes us equal, it's love. Passion. Desire. You made me yours instinctively, without even knowing you were doing it. I intend to make you mine." I didn't reply, for his mouth was suddenly on mine, hot and hard. Wrapping my arms around his neck, I pressed closer, the heat from him curling around us, joining with mine until I was sure we were going to go up in an inferno. I was all for it. What a way to go.

How he got my clothes off without me noticing, I'll never know. One minute I'd been pressed against him, desperate for more, and the next, I was totally naked. So was he.

He started to back us toward a wall, but I stopped him.

"No. The sofa." I pointed, and he changed direction, tossing me down. I bounced once, and he landed on top of me.

"Nice. I like this," He growled, moving to his knees.

"Don't get too comfy," I grinned.

"I thought it was my turn to mark you?" He arched an eyebrow, and I melted a little at the expression on his face.

"Oh, it is. You're going to love it, don't you worry." I rolled us without warning so that he was flat on his back on the sofa.

"I do think you could be right, devil woman." He grinned wolfishly, and a thrill of delight shot through me.

Then his mouth was on my neck, and I felt it, the puncture of his teeth in my flesh. I didn't think anything could ever top this feeling, his mark weaving its magic through me, as his fire demon heat coursed through my veins, filling me, completing me.

His tongue gently laved the wound on my neck before his mouth found its way back to mine, and I tasted my own blood on his lips.

We were as one.

TWELVE

"Finished?"

I squealed when Dacian's voice suddenly came from behind the sofa.

"Get out!" I ordered, sitting up and waving a hand toward my office door.

"No. We've got important business to discuss." He shrugged, apparently unconcerned that he'd just walked in on us having sex. "And yes, Ash told me you two were getting it on in here. I waited until you were done."

"We're not done," I protested.

"Wrong," he retorted "you're done. For now."

My cheeks heated when I realized that, of course, we had been heard. I hadn't exactly been quiet.

"Come on, babe, I'm pretty sure Dacian wouldn't have interrupted if it wasn't important. Right?" Levi stood unashamedly naked and eyeballed Dacian.

Dacian held his gaze, nodding. "Correct."

"Well, just get out while I get dressed," I grumbled. Dacian opened his mouth, but I cut him off. "Don't even say it! Out!" Without looking at Levi, I tossed him his pants. "Get dressed."

Now that I had business to discuss with Dacian, Levi's nakedness was a distraction. Quickly pulling on my own clothes, I wondered what had brought Dacian to Hell. To interrupt us the way he had, it had to be important. Was Heaven in worse shape than any of us realized? Was it crumbling altogether? Worry replaced the euphoria of moments before. I looked at Levi, a sadness in my heart. Everything was wonderful, and not at the same time. He was taking all of this remarkably well —discovering he'd changed into a fire demon, that he was marked and bound to me. How could he be so calm?

"Everything will be okay." He squeezed my hand in a comforting gesture.

"Of course it will." I faked a smile. A heavy sense of foreboding crept over me, and I had to physically shake my shoulders to shrug it off.

"Come on in, Dacian," I called, eager to get this over with. Whatever the problem was, we'd deal with it.

"From what Ash just told me, you already know the displaced souls are starting to return to Earth as revenants," Dacian said, striding into the room.

Levi and I were standing by the sofa. I bit back a laugh when I saw Dacian eye it, then veer toward my desk instead.

"Yes, we're aware." Following him, I took my seat behind the desk. Levi sank down into one of the chairs opposite. Dacian claimed the chair next to him, leaning forward to rest his elbows on his knees.

"Well, there are a whole lot more. Thousands. We can't lose their souls, Lucy. It feels like murder, sitting back and doing nothing."

I nodded. "We need to force Michael and Gabriel to open the Pearly Gates." Easier said than done. My brothers were stubborn fools and didn't seem to give a damn about the souls under their care.

"That's not a viable option anymore," Dacian muttered.

"Oh?"

"Heaven is too unstable. It's not safe." Dacian was looking at the floor, but I could feel the worry emanating from him.

"Fuck." Flopping back in my chair, I stared at the ceiling as if the answers to our problems could be found there. "We need to find Dad. He can fix Heaven and open the Gates."

"Yes, but we have absolutely no fucking idea where he is." Dacian's voice was sharp, and I snapped my eyes to him. "Sorry. I know Heaven isn't your jurisdiction. But..."

"It's okay, Dacian. You're right. We need to save the souls. Dad is important, but he will have to wait a little bit longer while we deal with this situation first. And I have a plan." It bothered me that searching for Dad kept getting pushed further and further back.

"You do?" Levi and Dacian said in unison.

I nodded. "We'll bring them to Hell. Temporarily."

"But they haven't sinned," Dacian protested.

"They won't be treated as sinners," I assured him. "I'll create a new zone for them. They'll be comfortable here until we can sort out the mess in Heaven."

"You'd do that?"

"Yes. Of course. If it's not safe for them in Heaven, then Hell, it will have to be. But while I organize their accommodations, I need you to do something for me."

"Name it." Dacian scooted forward on his chair, making me smile. He was so keen, so eager to help. It was an excellent quality to have. My father chose well with him.

"I need you to deal with the remaining revenants on Earth. As we speak, I'm sure more are falling."

"Yes. Dozens every minute." He shook his head before running his fingers through his hair, leaving the strands in tousled disarray. "I'll go now. Is there anything else?"

"Nope. Let me get some things in place here, and then we'll move the souls in. How many do you think?"

"Twenty to thirty-thousand, maybe more."

"Okay." I hid my dismay. That was a lot of souls, and moving them here would require space I didn't have readily available. But for every problem, there was always a solution. Waving him off, I called for Ashliel.

"You rang?" Her heels clicked across the floor before coming to a stop beside my desk.

"We're going to do a dimension expansion," I told her.

"We are?" The excitement in her voice was unmistakable. "Cool! I've been waiting for this day!"

"I'll bet. Can you get everything in place? Alert the guards, put everyone on lockdown?"

"I'm on it. I'll open the chamber, too."

"Thank you." I watched her leave, my mind on the task ahead.

"So, what's a dimension expansion?" Levi interrupted my train of thought.

"I'm going to make Hell bigger. We need more space if we're going to house thirty thousand souls. I'm going to create a new zone, just for them, to keep them away from the sinners."

"You can do that?" His eyes were round in his face.

"Yup. This is the first time I've had to do it, though. That's why Ashliel is excited. She knew we would reach capacity soon, and a massive influx like this has just sped it up."

"And the chamber? What's that?"

"It's like a panic room for magic. It'll take a lot of power to do this, and I can't have any of it leaking out. I need to keep Hell safe while I do this."

"So you use a dimension expansion...spell?"

"Correct."

"Can anyone do it?"

"No. Only a select few."

"Your brothers?"

"They're Arch Angels as well, so yes, they can. But not in my dimension. They have no power here." I stood, pushing my chair back, and held out my hand to Levi. "I need to prepare. This is big. It's going to take a lot of energy."

He frowned, linking his fingers with mine. "It's safe, isn't it? You're not going to get hurt?"

"A little drained, maybe. Tired. But I'll be okay."

Hand in hand, we crossed to the elevator and rode up to the penthouse. The doors slid open, and I had to tug Levi across the threshold, for he stood in the doorway with his mouth hanging open.

"This. Is. Amazing," he breathed, finally stepping forward. He dropped my hand and crossed to the wall of windows overlooking Hell. I watched him as he wandered the expanse of my home, taking in its sleek, modern surfaces, the external glass walls, and black marble floors.

"I need to shower."

That caught his attention. He turned with a leer on his face. "Need me to help?"

Laughing, I shook my head. "No, but thanks for the offer. I need to conserve my energy, and showering with you results in the exact opposite." I waved my hand around my open plan living room, kitchen, and dining area. "Make yourself at home. I won't be long."

My bedroom was twice the size of Levi's entire apartment back on Earth. It, too, had glass walls. The view stole my breath, even after all this time. Below was my city, the one I'd built from the ground up. The black buildings rose majestically, towering over the streets, silhouetted against a stunning sky of purples, pinks, and oranges. Hell boasted a perpetual sunset. No blue skies here. In the distance, mountains marked the northern boundary of Hell. In the south, flat plains of wasteland, an orange desert where survival was impossible. To the east was an ocean, its white waters deceptively beautiful, but if you were to touch it, the acid levels would melt your flesh from your bones in seconds. And finally, to the west, a sheer drop to nothing. A bottomless pit that went on for all of eternity. And Hell HQ was balanced on the edge of it.

I flicked on the taps in the bathroom and stood beneath the shower, letting the water pound down on me. I had to remove all traces of Levi from my flesh. I was going to be drawing heavily on my magic, and it needed to be pure. Strong. I'd downplayed how hard this was going to be. As

Hell's dimensions stretched, I had to take care not to destroy what was already here. One wrong move, and I might inadvertently flood the city with a tsunami of the acid ocean. Or the mountains could explode, creating landslides. Or HQ—and the whole city, for that matter—could topple into the never-ending abyss. Yeah, no pressure at all.

Calming my thoughts, I closed my eyes and focused on centering my energy. The spell would come to me instinctively once I was in the chamber, but preparation was key, and I had to be calm and focused. All my worries about Levi, my brothers, and my dad had to stop. And, just like everyone else, I didn't have a switch that could turn it all off. Although that would be cool. I made a mental note to talk to Dad about making that an addition to the next generation of humans. An upgrade.

"Focus," I scolded myself, dragging in a deep breath, holding it, and blowing it out.

I wasn't sure how long I stayed in the shower, meditating, but my fingers were pruned when I finally turned off the water. Wrapping myself in a black silk robe, I waved my hand to dry my hair, leaving it loose down my back, then stepped barefoot into the living room. Levi was still at the bank of windows, his hands pressed against the glass.

"The mountains look really close like I could reach out and touch them," he said, hearing me come up behind him. "But I'm guessing that's just an illusion?"

"You got it. It would take you, oh, about a year in a high-speed car to reach them."

"And the desert?"

"Same. And the ocean. The only thing that's as close as it seems is the precipice we're perched on."

"Fuck!" He raced across the room, looking out the opposite windows to the drop below. "How do we not fall? Do you have earthquakes here? How can this be safe?"

"It's safe because I keep it safe." I shrugged. "Come on. We need to go. Ashliel should have the chamber ready by now." Levi reached for my hand, but I snatched it away. "Sorry. No touching. I need to keep my energy pure."

"So I can't kiss you for good luck?"

"As much as I wish you could? You can't."

As he mulled this over, we silently stepped into the elevator. I commanded it to deliver us to the chamber, and mere seconds later, we arrived. The doors slid open, and Levi followed me out. Ashliel greeted us.

"We're all set." She was practically vibrating with excitement, her hair dancing around her head in bright red flames. I chuckled. She was like a kid in a candy shop.

The chamber was different from anything else in Hell. While all the buildings were modern and sleek, this room was a reflection of eras long past. The walls were hewn from rock, chiseled by hand, and far from smooth. Lush rugs were scattered across the stone floor. Lamps lit the room, and in the center of it was a pentagram with a candle at each point.

"Is this a cave?" Levi asked, wandering around the room. I nodded, waiting for him to work it out. It didn't take long. "We're in the mountains, aren't we? A cave in the mountains?"

"We are," I confirmed.

"But...we took the elevator."

"We did."

"But how?"

"Magic." The elevator could take me anywhere I wanted to go within this realm. If I wanted to be in the middle of the white ocean, it would deliver me there. I just had to command it. Only Ashliel and I had that power.

"Is this why there are mountains in Hell? Is this where it all started?"

"Yup. We had to clear some land, level some parts, move others. Think of it like working with clay, molding it into what we wanted it to be."

"We? You helped God?"

"He did most of the work. I assisted with the big stuff but left the finer details to Dad. He's a details man."

"Okay, enough chit-chat." Ashliel clapped her hands. "Time to do this! Levi, sit over there, and don't speak, don't touch anything, and don't interrupt in any way."

"Right." He crossed to a pile of throw pillows on the floor and sank down, cross-legged, to watch.

Ashliel handed me an ancient book. We took care not to touch as I accepted it from her.

"Ready?" she asked, her breath hitching.

"Can you light the candles for me?"

I crossed to stand in the center of the pentagram, the book in my hands. The candles snapped to life around me, blazing high before settling into a steady flame. Closing my eyes, I held both palms out in front of me, the closed book balanced on them. In my mind, I called forth the spell, and the book flipped open, the pages turning until settling into silence.

Opening my eyes, I read the text in front of me, nodded, and closed the book. It disappeared, and I heard Levi gasp. Blocking him out, I closed my eyes again and began the spell, picturing in my mind the new zone, building it brick by brick, pushing back the shores of the white sea.

Raising my hands, I felt a pulse of energy between them and knew it was red and sparkling without having to look at it. Gently, I began to stretch it, push it, pull it, making it bigger. The cave trembled, dust drifting down from the roof, and I paused as sweat beaded on my upper lip. *Slowly*, I cautioned myself. *Do this slowly, or Hell will crumble.*

Inch by inch, I worked at expanding the dimension, rolling out acres of green fields along the foreshore of the white sea. Upon the fields, I placed tall buildings, this time made of white marble, replicas of the black marble buildings in the rest of Hell. The skyscrapers continued to appear, and I continued to sweat, my body trembling. I forced myself to push on. The displaced souls deserved this, and I was determined to give them a temporary home that was as similar to Heaven as I could create. Golden gates appeared on the path to the new zone.

They slammed shut and locked, keeping the zone safe from the rest of Hell.

"She's bleeding." I heard Levi's voice in the distance, then Ashliel shushing him with, "It's just a nose bleed; she'll be fine."

I was almost done. The major stuff was complete. I'd made space, created a new zone with green grass and white buildings fit for the souls. Over fifty high-rise buildings lined the shoreline, and streets of golden bricks wove around them. Smaller buildings housed shops and amenities. A swimming pool. A movie theatre. Restaurants. Now it was time for the final touches—furnishing and decorating the apartments I'd created.

I was tiring, growing weak, and couldn't spend the time I would have liked to make them all individual and perfect; instead, with a sweep of my hand, a palette of rose gold and white flooded over the buildings, followed by a soft grey palette for the beds, sofas, and tables. It would have to do. I made a mental note to get Ashliel to visit each and every soul and take requests for items I'd missed. This was to be their temporary Heaven, and as much as I wanted it to be perfect, my magic was fading, my strength all but gone.

I fell to my knees, slumping on the floor.

"Lucy!" Levi shouted.

"No! She has to close out of the spell. Don't touch her!"

I heard shuffling and knew Ashliel had restrained Levi, stopping him from coming to me. She was right. I muttered the words that would end the spell, shooting a sonic boom through the cave that knocked me on my back. The candles and lamps went out, plunging us into darkness. Seconds later, they flickered back to life, and Ashliel stood over me, offering me her hand.

"That was fucking awesome!" She beamed, then, as an afterthought, added, "You okay?"

I nodded, letting her pull me to my feet. My hair was damp with sweat, my nose still dripped blood, and I felt about as strong as a limp noodle. Then Levi was there, swinging me up into his arms. Ordinarily, I would have protested, but at this point, I was too damn tired—and I was secretly grateful that I didn't have to hold my own body weight.

"Lucy?" Ashliel's worried voice penetrated my foggy brain. "What's that?"

Turning my head to look where she was pointing, I could see what appeared to be fabric protruding from the rock.

"Put me down," I said to Levi, staggering as he

set me back on my feet. Crossing to the wall, I touched the fabric, rubbing it between my fingers, giving it a tug to see if it would come loose. It didn't.

"It looks like...but it couldn't be."

"What? What is it?" Ashliel clasped my forearm.

"It looks like Dad's robes," I whispered.

THIRTEEN

"He's here? In Hell?" Ashliel's voice was barely a whisper. "How? And where? Like, is he in the rock?"

"Shh." Placing both my palms against the rock wall, I closed my eyes and concentrated. "There's something here."

"God?" Ashliel asked.

"No. I can sense him, but there's something between him and us."

"The rock?" Ashliel gestured at the wall as if the answer was obvious.

"No, Ash. You don't think God could move the rock on his own? There's something else. Something powerful."

"Oh. Yeah, right, makes sense."

Ignoring her, I continued to stand with my hands against the rock face, pushing my energy into it, feeling it rebound at me.

"Stand back."

I waited until Levi and Ashliel had stepped away, then swept my hands through the air, red magic swirls sparking from my hands. The rock face began to crumble away, the clatter of falling rubble echoing throughout the chamber. Coughing, I waved the dust from my face and tucked my nose into the crook of my elbow to stop from breathing it in.

"It's a door," Levi said when the dust had settled. "A pretty impressive-looking one, at that. Is it made from steel?"

We all moved closer to examine it. It had to be at least ten feet tall and five feet wide. On the inner border was a plain raised edge framing the door. In the center, there was a symbol—a dragon within a circle. There was no handle. But more of the fabric I was sure belonged to Dad's robe poked through the edge, caught between the door and the frame.

"It's a seal." Ashliel was running her fingers over the dragon symbol. "I've heard of them but never seen one."

"A seal?" I reached out and touched the door, running my hands over it.

"Seriously, Lucy, did you not read the instruction manual for this place?" Ashliel tossed her flaming hair over her shoulder, her face revealing her exasperation.

"Of course I read it." I couldn't lie. I had read it—once when she'd first put it together for me. But did I remember any of it? That was the question she should have been asking.

Because the answer to that was no, I did not. I'd been too busy managing the day-to-day of Hell to remember all of its little intricacies and nuances. It seemed Ashliel hadn't forgotten any of it, though, and that was why I hired her in the first place—and loved her for the friend she was.

"Remind me," I prompted.

After blowing out a breath, she spoke almost without breathing. "There are four seals, each represented by a horse. The white horse will release the white horseman, who symbolizes pestilence. He will rain down disease and plague on the earth. The red horse will release the red horseman, who symbolizes war. He will unleash mass slaughter on the earth. The black horse will release the black horseman, who symbolizes famine. The earth will starve. And finally, the rider on the pale horse will bring death."

"Wait," Levi said once she'd run out of steam. "So what you're saying is, if we break this seal to open the door, we'll be releasing one of the horsemen? He's in there?"

"The horseman isn't behind the door," I replied, "but the act of breaking the seal will call him forth."

"Why create the horsemen in the first place? Who did it? And why?"

I shrugged. "A safeguard."

"Okay, so you think God is behind the door?"

I looked at the ratty piece of fabric poking out between the door and the frame. "I think he just might be," I said sadly. "He's been missing all this time, and we've only just noticed. What sort of daughter am I that I didn't notice my dad was missing for thousands of years?" Tears coursed down my cheeks as a wave of emotion, both powerful and debilitating, pounded through me.

"You were busy." Levi was only trying to help, but his words were hollow. *I was busy*. What sort of fucking excuse was that? I was worse than the humans. I should be burning in the pit for my neglect.

"Lucy, you didn't notice because your brothers

covered it up, remember? You still got messages from Heaven. They let you believe they were coming from God. You are not responsible for this," Ashliel pointed out.

"But he's *here*. In *my* realm. And I didn't know."

"That's it exactly. You didn't know." Levi pulled me against his chest. I let him hold me, soothing my raw emotions.

"Yeah, well, you two can stand around all sooky la la and shit, but in the meantime, we've got God trapped behind a seal," Ashliel snapped. "I think that's more important than your *feelings*."

I sucked in a breath, shocked at Ashliel's harsh words. My hurt must have shown on my face because she threw up her hands. "What? I always have and always will say it like it is! Don't wimp out on me now, Lucifer. Get your shit together. It's not like you to be all *emotional* like this." She said the word like it was poison on her tongue.

Levi stiffened, then growled, "Back off!"

"No. No, she's right. I don't know why I feel so incredibly emotional right now, but she's right. Let's focus. If we break the seal, we'll be putting a chain of events in motion that no man, angel, demon, or god can halt. Or so they say."

"So they say?" Levi sounded surprised. "So you

don't even know if that's true? About the seals and the horsemen?"

"Let's go back to the office and do some research. Let's try and find out exactly what we're dealing with here, how we break the seal, and what the repercussions will be if any." It pained me to leave, but expanding the dimension had tired me, and what I'd said was true—we were all just guessing at what was going on here. Except for Ashliel, I was pretty sure her database of a brain had pulled up the correct information. We just had to dig a little deeper to get all the answers.

"Agreed," she said, leading the way back to the elevator.

We were standing in my office moments later. Levi crossed to the window and admired the view of the new zone while Ashliel slipped into my chair and began typing something at my console. As an afterthought, she said, without looking at me, "You might want to get cleaned up. You've got blood all over your face, and your robe is filthy."

"Oh. Right." Glancing down, I realized she was right. The black silk robe I'd worn to the chamber was covered in dust and had damp spots of blood down the front where my nose had bled. I debated for a second. Go shower and dress, or use my magic?

The shower was very tempting, but time was of the essence, so with a wave of my hand, I cleaned myself up. I was dressed in black leather pants and a red halter top in seconds, my hair once more in pristine condition and falling in waves down my back.

"Urgh. Shouldn't have used my magic." I clutched my stomach, a wave of nausea rolling through me.

Levi was by my side in a micro-second. "You okay?" With his arm around my waist, he guided me to the sofa, and I flopped down, less than graceful.

"Must have used too much magic today. I just need to rest. I'll be fine."

"Is there anything I can do? How do you replenish magic?" Sitting by my side, he clasped my hand in his, worry evident on his face.

"Rest is all I need," I assured him.

"I've never seen you pale before."

That caught Ashliel's attention, and she swiveled to eyeball me. "He's right. Shit, you look awful. Pale, with a hint of...green?" She cocked her head, considering. "Yeah, definitely green. So, this is what happens when you use mofo amounts of magic. Interesting. I'll make a note." Turning back to the keyboard, she continued typing.

I chuckled. When Ashliel said she'd make a note,

that was precisely what she'd do—add it to the Hell Handbook, which was now several tomes in length.

"Found anything yet?" I asked her.

"Kinda," she muttered, her head moving up and down as she read the screen, then typed, over and over.

I was exhausted watching her, so I shut my eyes and let my head rest against the back of the sofa. I'd never felt so wiped out in my life. I was almost totally drained of magic, and I didn't like it, not one bit. Thankfully, I wouldn't need to increase Hell's dimensions again any time soon. Once we got Dad out from behind the door, he'd get Heaven back in order, retrieve his lost souls, and I could convert the new zone into prison quarters, as I'd initially intended to do with that part of Hell. While that would require some magic, it would be nowhere near as much as I'd used today.

I must have dozed for a little while, for I jumped in surprise when Ashliel announced, "Got it!"

"You do?" I sat up, running my hands over my face and smoothing back my hair. I felt marginally better. My magic was returning.

"I think this is the first seal. It was created when this dimension was being made. There's no way anyone would have gotten it past God otherwise.

Whoever made it must have used the first seal to trap God, then went on their merry way creating as many as they liked."

"How many seals are we talking about?" Levi asked.

Ashliel shrugged, "Seven are documented, but there could be more."

Seven. But Ashliel had only initially known about four. Who had set these seals?

"And how do we break the seal?" I asked. "What happens when we do?"

"According to this—" She indicated the screen. "This is the first seal which, when broken, will release the first horseman. The first horseman rides a white horse and will release disease and plague on Earth."

"Why on Earth? Why not here, where the seal is?" I asked.

"Because these have been set up specifically to target—and hurt—God. And disease and plague are not going to harm you or your demons. But they will hurt the humans, and they are just as precious to God."

"Man, someone sure must hate him," Levi muttered, shaking his head.

I noticed she hadn't answered the first part of my question. "How do we break it, Ashliel?"

"We need the blood of a righteous man."

"Well, that's easy." Levi cut across the silence that followed. "I'll do it. My blood should work."

"This is fucking weird," I muttered.

"How everything is falling into place, almost like it was planned?" Ashliel asked. "Yeah. It is."

"Bit of a long-term plan, don't you think?" Levi said. "You'd have to be okay with a slow game, waiting thousands of years for it to play out."

"Do you think Destiny and Fate are involved?" Ashliel asked. "They're good at this end-game bullshit."

"That's what I'm worried about. I thought they were Dad's allies. They had a lot of input in creating Earth. Was it all a setup? And if it was, are they behind it? Or someone else?"

"You know the best person to ask?" Ashliel stood by the door, waiting.

"Dad." I rose to my feet. We had to get Dad out of the prison he'd been locked in for thousands of years. Only he had the answers we needed.

"Wait!" Levi jumped up and grabbed my wrist. "You're talking about destiny and fate and all that, but what if we're playing into their hands? What if this is exactly what they want you to do? What if God isn't even behind that door? What if it's a trick? Or a trap?"

"It's his robe. I'm one hundred percent sure of it," I argued.

"It could have been planted," Levi pointed out.

"It could have, I agree. But there's only one way to know for sure—break the seal and open the door."

FOURTEEN

Breaking the seal was deceptively simple. Levi sliced his palm open with a knife and placed it over the dragon symbol. I'd expected some sort of fanfare, the sound of something breaking, at the very least, but there was nothing. No lights flashing, no boom or even the sound of a lock clicking open. Zero. Nada. Zilch. The door remained closed.

"Did it work?" Ashliel bounced from foot to foot, impatient.

"I don't know. Did you feel anything?" I asked Levi, who still had his hand pressed to the door.

He shook his head. "Nope. Didn't feel a thing. Maybe it didn't break. Maybe it's not my blood it needs."

"Wait, wait!" Ashliel exclaimed. "Breaking the seal doesn't mean the door will open. It just means we can open the door."

"What?" I frowned. What was she on about?

"We have to open the door. It won't happen on its own. As in, PUSH!"

She pressed her palms against the right-hand side of the door and threw her weight into it. Levi joined her, placing his hands above hers, and sure enough, it started to move, groaning and screeching in protest. I joined them, and with the three of us pushing, the door slowly swung inwards.

The room inside was pitch black. I wasn't sure if it was out of instinct or what, but Ashliel and Levi automatically took a step backward. I stood frozen in the doorway, letting my eyes adjust to the darkness. No horseman came flying out to trample us beneath the hooves of his steed, but then, we'd known the horseman wasn't physically behind the seal. If the stories were true, we'd just released him upon the earth. I'd deal with that later, but for now, I had to see if my father was in this room.

Taking a breath, I stepped inside and almost screamed when something touched my foot. Glancing down, I saw...was that a hand? An almost skeletal hand resting on top of my foot.

"Dad?" Falling to my knees, I clasped the hand, running my fingers up past the wrist to the forearm, then the elbow, then up to the shoulder and across, to the head and face. In the dim light, I saw the mummified face of my father. "Oh, Dad." Tears rolled down my cheeks, dropping onto us both.

"Is he in there?" I heard Ashliel say, but I was too choked up to answer. I'd found my dad, but it was too late. Bowing my head, I clasped the bony hand between my own, raised it to my lips, and pressed a kiss to the dried-up skin.

"I'm so sorry," I whispered, my heart breaking.

Someone had trapped him here all those years ago, and I hadn't known. Hadn't known he was here in this tomb of darkness, slowly withering away to nothing. Only he wasn't nothing, was he? It dawned on me that he should have been a pile of dust at the worst or a pile of bones at best. But he was still in one piece, sitting up against the wall. Maybe he wasn't dead. I allowed hope to blossom in my chest, and to test my theory, I sent a bit of magic into him.

It was all he needed. His flesh filled out ever so slightly, and he moved just a fraction, then a little more. I gave him some more magic, careful not to deplete myself, as I wasn't fully recovered from stretching the dimension. What I hadn't anticipated was the man's instinct for survival. Before I could pull away or stop him, he'd caught my hands in his bony grasp and began sucking the magic from me in great, gulping waves.

"Dad!" I gasped, feeling it ripping away, draining me, dangerously so. "Dad, stop!"

"Lucy?" I heard Levi's voice, saw his shadow falling over us as he stood in the doorway, tried to turn my head to look at him, but I was so weak.

"Levi..." I was hemorrhaging magic, my power draining too fast. I couldn't sustain it or myself. The world spun. I could feel myself falling, then nothing—nothing but darkness.

***

"She's waking up."

I groaned, fighting to open my eyes, but it was too difficult. Wearily, I rubbed a hand over my face. Since when had my arms gotten so heavy? They flopped bonelessly to my side.

"What happened?" Surely that croaking noise wasn't my voice?

"Your dad. He drained you." Levi was by my side, his hand clasping mine.

I pried my eyes open with the utmost effort and

squinted at him. "Right. We found him." My lips split into a semblance of a smile. A smile Levi didn't return. Instead, he looked...pissed off. "What?" I asked.

"We found him, all right. He drained you to heal himself, then left."

"What? He's gone?" I struggled to sit up but could barely control my limbs. Levi pressed a finger into my shoulder to hold me down, indicating how weak I was.

"Relax. You need to heal. He almost killed you."

"Where did he go?"

Levi was right. I was weaker than I'd ever been, dangerously so. I was vulnerable. This whole situation was dangerous, and again, I couldn't help but wonder if my brothers were involved. Was this their attempt to overthrow me and take over Hell? They certainly wanted to dominate something, and since their attempt on Earth had failed, was Hell next? Trap Dad, knowing that when I found him, he'd need my magic to heal himself?

"Ashliel?" I croaked.

"She's busy," Levi told me. "She's organizing extra patrols and monitoring from your office."

"Good. But you didn't answer my question. Where did Dad go?"

"He muttered something about Lilith and disappeared."

I closed my eyes, thinking, although it was difficult to focus on anything. My mind was so foggy. Dad had said Mom's name—Lilith. Was she involved, or had he said it because he'd spent his years in captivity thinking about her? Thinking about how much he loved her and missed her. Wanting her back, maybe.

"I have an idea." Levi's voice interrupted my thoughts. I opened my eyes to glance up at him. "Let me give you some of my magic to help heal you. I don't like seeing you like this."

"You don't have magic. You're human," I protested, closing my eyes again. So tired. So very, very tired.

"I'm a fire demon, remember? You bound me. I'm yours. You're mine. You've healed me before. Now let me heal you."

His words sounded like they were coming from a distance. I was fading, but I clung to what he was saying, trying to claw my way back from the darkness. He'd said something about a fire demon, but we didn't have fire demons in Hell. Did we? I was confused.

What was happening to me?

Warm lips pressed against my own. Lips I recognized, even in my dazed state. These lips were hot, just the way I liked it, and I automatically granted him access, although why he was kissing me when I was practically comatose, I had no idea.

Then I felt it—the tendrils of fire that swirled around my mouth, down my throat, splitting off into a thousand different directions and burning through my body. It was ambrosia. I couldn't get enough! Grabbing his head with both hands, I devoured him, my tongue dueling with his while his kiss revived me.

"Enough!" he gasped, pulling away.

I growled a protest, but he caught my wrists and held firm. Opening my eyes, I knew the flames of Hell were dancing in my gaze. I could see them reflected in Levi's eyes.

"Better?" he asked, cocking his head to one side.

"Much!" His fire had saved me. I wasn't at full strength yet, but I was functioning. He'd jump-started my magic, just enough that it could begin repairing itself. Without my magic, I'd not only been dying, but I'd been empty inside. There had been a void where it was ripped away, but now it was returning, almost the same as it was, but now there was something different. Had my magic changed because Levi had infused it with his own?

Sitting up, I swung my legs off the edge of the bed and stood. The room didn't spin or sway, and I actually felt normal. But I also felt changed.

"Thank you," I said. Levi had stood with me, and I placed a hand against his cheek. "For saving me."

"My pleasure." His grin was warm and inviting, and I was tempted, so tempted, to toss him down on the bed and ravish him. But Ashliel was keeping Hell safe. She'd known the realm was in danger with me out of action. So rather than toss Levi onto the bed, I laced my fingers with his and tugged him after me.

"No reward then?" he teased as I led him out of my bedroom and toward the elevator.

"Oh, there'll be a reward." I winked, stepping into the elevator and pulling him into my arms for a kiss as it sped us to Hell HQ. It took all of one second, so the kiss was far from satisfying, but each touch of Levi's skin fueled my magic. The feeling was sinfully delicious.

"Good, you're up." Ashliel was standing in front of the multi-screen display of Earth, her eyes darting from one to the next, monitoring the situation.

"I am. What's happening?"

"Well, your dad bailed." She pouted, arms folded

across her chest, clearly affronted. "I mean, we found him, and you almost died saving him, and he couldn't be bothered with a thank-you. He didn't even hang around to check that you were okay. He just left." She snapped her fingers, indicating he'd disappeared into thin air.

"Levi told me." I tried not to let my hurt filter through into my voice, but I suspected it was there, anyway, from the glance Ashliel gave me.

"He said her name," she replied.

I nodded. "Lilith."

"Who's Lilith?" Levi asked.

"My mom."

"Your mom is Lilith? Isn't she...evil?"

"You've been reading the wrong books," I told him, shaking my head. "So many crazy stories were made up about my mother. She isn't evil. She was just...lonely. She and Dad fell in love, then Dad got obsessed with his creations, and...well, he neglected her. Ignored her for long periods. Eventually, her love died, and she took off."

"Without her children." It wasn't a question.

I shrugged. "I don't know why she didn't take us. Maybe she thought we'd be happier in Heaven. Or maybe she had nowhere to go and no way to provide for us. I'm not judging her, and neither should you."

He heard it. The tone in my voice. The one that said I would kick his ass if he dissed my mother. It was a touchy subject. I barely remembered her. She'd left when I was four years old. And yes, I'd missed her, had cried myself to sleep more often than I wanted to admit, but that wasn't to say I grew up without love. Dad loved me; I had no doubt about that. The one thing that concerned me right now, though, was why he had left so suddenly. And why did he say Mom's name?

"We've got incoming," Ashliel said.

"Who?" Standing by her side, I examined the monitors. Then I spotted him. "Dacian," we said in unison.

"Let him in," I told her, pacing as I waited for the Seraph angel to arrive. I didn't have to wait long.

"He's back, God's back!" Dacian said as he entered the room.

"We know," Levi drawled from his position on the sofa.

"What? How?" Dacian seemed disappointed we hadn't been all over him for details. I bit my lip, not knowing how to feel. I thought I'd be brimming with excitement that we'd found Dad, but his behavior—well, his immediate departure, to be precise—had me puzzled and not a little bit hurt.

"Because we found him here and rescued him."

"Oh." Deflated, Dacian lowered himself onto the sofa, taking the corner opposite Levi.

I recommenced my pacing. "What did he say? Did he tell you what happened?" I asked.

"No. But word spread quickly through Heaven that he'd returned. The streets were packed. I couldn't get near Angel Towers." He shrugged. "So I came here instead. The new zone looks great, by the way."

I knew Dacian was trying to soothe my ruffled feathers and distract me from the sting of what I'd taken to be my fathers' rejection. It kind of worked.

"Yeah, I'm really pleased with how it turned out. Too bad I have to change it, though."

"Oh?"

"Well, sinners aren't going to get five-star luxury and beach-front views." Crossing to the window, I looked out at the stunning white buildings I'd created. It wouldn't take much to modify them. A thought occurred to me. "Are the Pearly Gates open?"

"Yeah, and Heaven is healing. Everywhere God walked looks good as new."

"Good. That's good." All those lost souls were no longer lost, and Dacian had taken care of the ones that had fallen. Now the only problem we had left was the white horseman we'd unleashed on Earth.

"Any sign of the horseman?" I asked Ashliel, not taking my attention from the window.

"Nope. I went back over the seconds when we broke the seal to see if I could identify any activity, but so far, nothing."

"Maybe it isn't true. Maybe the horsemen don't exist," I suggested hopefully.

"Maybe, but why put them in the book?"

"I don't know. None of this is making sense." Then another thought hit me. "Fuck!" I exclaimed. "Mr. Meow. We've left Mr. Meow alone."

"Relax," Ashliel said. "Time moves differently, remember? To that cat, you've only been gone a little while. He'll be fine."

She had a point. He would be fine. He was most likely asleep and hadn't even noticed Levi's absence. But still, I felt like we'd abandoned Levi's life on Earth. His shop. His home. His pet. A strong hand wrapped around the nape of my neck and squeezed, making me jump.

"Why are you worried about my cat?" Levi murmured in my ear.

I shrugged. "I don't know. I just...I like your cat. It makes me sad to think of him there alone."

"Let's go back, then. All of this mess—" He waved his hand around. "—seems to have been resolved. God has returned, Heaven is open for business, and it appears the four horsemen are a myth. How about a little vacation Earth-side?"

Oh, it sounded appealing. So, so appealing. I was tired, and time out relaxing with Levi in his home was the perfect solution.

"Go!" Ashliel instructed. "I've got everything under control here. I'll see to the alterations of the new zone, keep an eye out for any horsemen, and will let you know if anything changes."

"See? Ash has it all in hand. What do you say?" Levi snuggled in behind me and nuzzled my ear, making me giggle.

"Okay, fine." I gave in, but it hadn't been much of a battle.

"Let me know if anything changes, though, okay?" I glanced at Ashliel.

She nodded. "Of course. Now go. You need to finish healing. I can feel your energy, and it's all off."

"Is that what that is?" Dacian spoke up. I'd forgotten he was there, still sprawled on the sofa.

"God drained her to save himself," Levi growled,

his annoyance apparent. "I gave her some of my magic before she fucking died."

"You have magic now?" Dacian was clearly confused.

"He's a fire demon!" Ashliel supplied, her voice once more edged with excitement at this turn of events.

"What the hell?"

"Exactly!" She practically clapped her hands in glee.

"How did you become a fire demon?"

"She bit him!" Ashliel jumped in before either of us could answer, and I threw a smile at Levi, who shrugged as if to say, "Let her have it."

"What?"

"You know, claimed him as her mate? Surely you've heard of it, Dacian? I know your mind was wiped, but Lucy fixed all that."

"Yes, I've heard of it. I just didn't realize..."

"What?" I asked.

"Nothing." Dacian shook his head. "So, you marked him. And he...changed?"

"So now they're compatible," Ashliel said. "*More* compatible, I should say. Since he was human, he wouldn't have been able to stay in this dimension indefinitely. Now he can."

"And who decided he'd be a fire demon?"

"Fate or Destiny," Ashliel supplied. "Either one of the sisters. Man, they are amazing! I so want to meet them someday."

Shaking his head, Dacian looked at me intently. "She's right, though. Your energy is all…different."

I shrugged. "Probably because of Levi's magic, like he said. I'm not sure how it works. Maybe his magic will stay combined with mine, and I'll have a different energy signature forever, or maybe once my magic has fully returned, I'll be back to my old self."

"Speaking of, let's go." Levi gave me a squeeze, reminding me we had some R&R to catch up on.

"Call me if anything changes. Anything at all," I told them before taking Levi's hand and transporting us back to Earth.

FIFTEEN

We had three blissful, uninterrupted days on Earth—nights full of love and days spent hanging out in Levi's apartment, watching daytime TV, and snuggling with Mr. Meow. He was fine, and Ashliel had been right. To him, our absence had been momentary. It was our fourth evening on Earth, and we were in the diner enjoying a late lunch when the storm started to roll in.

"Check out those clouds!" Levi pressed his face against the window and looked first one way, then the other. Dark, heavy clouds laden with rain was rolling in from every direction.

"It's been a long time since I've enjoyed a storm." The atmosphere in Hell was consistent. We didn't have weather, just purple skies that never changed.

The bell above the door jangled as a man rushed in, bringing a gust of wind with him. Turning, he pushed with both hands to get the door closed again.

"Man, this one is going to be a doozy!" he exclaimed, running his hands over his hair to smooth down the strands. "Sophie, turn the radio on, would you, love? This came out of nowhere. I want to check the forecast."

Sophie, our ever-so-friendly waitress, picked up a remote and turned off the jukebox, then flipped on the small radio behind the counter. She slid it toward the man who'd just come in and said, "Tune it to what you want, Carl." Seemingly disinterested, she returned to fussing behind the counter.

Carl played with the radio, and I returned my attention to Levi just as a loud rumble of thunder shook the café.

"Wow." Levi's eyes grew huge. "That was kinda loud, huh?"

"Yeah." I agreed but didn't have much to go on since I hadn't experienced storms before. Whenever I was on Earth, and the weather turned bad, I'd just return to Hell. But now I had Levi and his cat to consider.

"Levi," I began but was interrupted by a loud clap of thunder and a fork of lightning that pierced the sky.

"Did you see that?" Levi jumped to his feet and cupped his hands around his eyes as he pressed his face against the window to get a better look at the darkness that had crept over Shadow Falls. "I've never seen anything like it before."

"What? A storm?" I was surprised. He'd been born on Earth; surely, he'd experienced weather variations before.

"No. The thunder clapped *before* the lightning strike. Thunder is the sound lightning makes, so how could the thunder come before the lightning?"

I shrugged, watching as fat raindrops began to fall from the sky, just a few at first before it became a heavy deluge. Lightning continued to light up the sky, and the roll and rumble of thunder were never-ending.

"Think this will last long?" I yelled over the noise.

"It rolled in so quickly, I'd expect it to leave quickly, too. It must be some fast-moving weather front. Hey, Carl, any news on this storm?" Levi raised his voice to call out to the man at the counter, who had his ear pressed to the radio.

Carl lifted his head and looked at us. "Nah, it's the weirdest thing. Not a single weather report is saying we have a storm."

"What? That can't be right."

Levi went to listen to the radio reports himself while I stayed near the window, watching. The sunny afternoon of moments ago had turned into early nightfall with the arrival of the storm clouds, and now, with the rain hammering down, visibility was near zero. From what I could see, the drains could no longer cope with the torrential downpour, and water was filling the street. Before my eyes, it rose to curb level, then began lapping onto the sidewalk.

"Sophie?" I called, keeping my eye on the rising water outside. "Do you have anything to block the door?"

"Block the door?" she repeated. Quickly casting a glance her way, I could see the confusion on her face and sighed. *So not helpful, Sophie.*

"What's up?" Carl asked.

"I think we might flood." I nodded outside, indicating the water creeping across the sidewalk toward the café doors.

"What? Oh my God! This can't be happening!" Sophie screeched, hysterical, rushing from one end of the counter to the other.

Ignoring the hysterical waitress, Carl and Levi hurried to the doors to look outside. What once was the street was now a lake.

"It's rising fast," Carl muttered.

"Too damn fast. A few tea towels shoved under the door aren't going to stop it. If we're going to get out of here, we need to go now." Levi was as calm as ever, and I loved him for it.

"Where do we go? The roads are impassable." Carl tried to match Levi's level of calm and almost convinced me he wasn't shit scared.

"We'll go to my place. It's around the corner, within walking distance. My apartment is on the first floor. We'll be safe there."

"Right. Good. Yes." Carl stood, nodding, and I bit back a grin.

"Sophie, turn everything off and come with us."

She looked at him, wild-eyed, but obeyed, flicking off switches, snatching up her bag, and flinging it over her shoulder before joining us by the front door. With the lights out, it was dark, and I briefly considered lighting the way. But I figured I'd hold off on exposing the humans to my magic until I absolutely had to.

"Ready?" Levi asked. We all nodded. Stepping forward, he pulled open the door, and the water lapped at the toe of his boot. "Looks like we're in luck. The water isn't that high yet. Got your keys, Sophie? We can lock up behind us."

By the time we'd exited the café and locked the doors, the water was around our ankles.

"Does it always rise this fast?" I asked, curious.

"It's never done this. Never rained this hard and never flooded," Levi told me over the roar of the falling rain. We were soaked to the bone, and our usual stroll to Levi's apartment took twice as long as we battled the wind that seemed intent on blowing us backward.

The water was up to our knees by the time we reached the fire escape at the rear of Levi's building. Pulling down the ladder, he helped everyone up, shouting encouragement as cold fingers slipped on the wet rungs. As we burst into Levi's apartment, leaving wet trails on the carpet, the lights began to flicker.

"Power's about to go out," Carl observed.

"Guys, the bathroom is in here," Levi said, pushing open the door and flicking the light switch.

"Grab some towels, dry off. Put the coffee pot on now if you want to try and beat the power outage. Lucy, can you come help me in the store? We'll grab some candles and see if we can't sandbag the front door with something."

"Sure."

Leaving Sophie and Carl in the apartment, I followed Levi downstairs to his shop. The water had seeped beneath the door and was continuing to trickle in. I could see it lapping about a foot high on the glass. With a quick burst of magic, I sealed the door, preventing any further water from entering.

"Want me to fix this?" I asked, indicating the ankle-deep water inside.

"Nah. It would look strange if my place was the only one that stayed dry. But I see you fixed the door?" He nodded his head at the water-tight seal I'd placed over the front of his shop.

"Yeah, I did."

"Let's put some stuff against the doors to make it look like we actually put effort into stopping the water, and magic wasn't involved."

I blew out a sigh. "If you insist." Following Levi's lead, I grabbed a roll of tape and began covering up the gaps while he piled up tapestries he'd pulled down from the walls.

"Does it really matter?" I asked, tearing the tape with my teeth.

"Does what matter?"

"This place. Hiding our magic. I mean, I get that this is your store, but are you going to return here... to this life?" It was a subject I'd been reluctant to broach, but since we'd bound ourselves to each other, we needed to act like semi-responsible adults and sort out our living arrangements.

Levi stopped and looked at me. "You're right." He laughed, the sound harsh, making me frown. "Why am I bothering? Remove your magic. Let the water in." He dropped the tapestry he was holding, and it splashed on the floor.

"Levi," I began, seeing he was upset.

He cut me off. "No, you're right. Why am I holding on to this life? This is the old me, the human me. This is what I built up with my grandmother. It has no standing now."

"Stop!" Rushing to him, I grabbed his wrists to prevent him from sweeping the contents of the counter onto the floor. "I'm sorry. I shouldn't have said anything. My timing is lousy, and I was wrong! This place is important. You built it with your grandmother. With love. Of course, that matters. I'm sorry."

Dripping wet and standing in ankle-deep water in his shop, we looked at each other. The storm continued to rage outside, wild and unabated, and I was pretty sure Levi's emotions were in similar turmoil.

"We'll work it out," I whispered, cupping his face in my hands and standing on tip-toes to kiss him. "For now, let's keep this place as safe as we can."

"Okay." Pressing a kiss to my forehead, he turned back to the counter, righting the items he'd knocked over, while I went back to kicking myself for being so insensitive. I'd gotten carried away and hadn't stopped to think that maybe Levi would miss his human life. Hell, I'd marked him, turned him into a fire demon without any consideration for what he wanted or how he'd feel about it. It had all been about me. A wave of shame swept over me, followed by self-doubt. What sort of person was I to do this to the man I loved?

"Whatever you're thinking, knock it off," Levi growled. He was now pulling items from the lower shelves and stacking them higher.

"What?"

"I can feel it. Your distress. It makes me itch. Can you stop beating yourself up about whatever it is you're beating yourself up over and just help me with the shop? Can you do that?"

"I can do that," I whispered, trying to stem the sting of hurt his cold words delivered. He was hurt and angry, and I was full of doubt and shame. What a pair.

"Lucy!" he snapped, and I immediately cast a magic bubble around myself, stopping any and all emotion from reaching him. The truth was, I couldn't turn it off. The way I felt, my emotions, weren't a tap. But I could stop them from affecting him, at least for a little while.

I thought I heard him whisper, "Thank fuck," but I couldn't be sure, so I let it go, instead concentrating on helping him get his shop ready for the flood.

When we were finished, he said, without looking at me, "Remove the magic keeping the water out."

"What? Why?"

"Because my shop flooding will make a plausible excuse as to why it's not open anymore. Why I decide to close up...for good."

"Are you sure?" I whispered, too scared to touch him for fear he'd lash out at me again.

"You were right. This life is over. I don't know

what's going to happen in the future, but I do know I'm not going back to reading tarot cards for a living."

"I'm sorry."

"Will you stop saying you're sorry and just do it? I'm pissed off and angry right now, but it's not with you, okay? So stop saying sorry. Every time you look at me with those sad eyes, you make me feel like I've kicked a puppy, and it hurts me that I'm hurting you. The two of us are just going around and around in a stupid loop hurting each other."

He took a deep breath. "The last three days here have been perfect. But we both know they were just a break from reality—our new reality—and this?" He waved his arm to indicate the shop. "This isn't part of it. There's only one thing I'm not negotiating on, and that's you. You complete me. Without you, I'm nothing, and I will not be apart from you. Ever."

I threw myself into his arms, tucking my face into his neck and squeezing. He returned my embrace, then pulled back a little. "Actually, there's two things."

"Oh?"

"Mr. Meow. He's family. We have to find a way to make this work for him, too. It may be selfish of me, but I don't want to give him up."

"Agreed." My heart practically exploded with affection for this man who would not abandon his cat, even for love.

We made our way back upstairs to find Sophie and Carl asleep. Sophie had passed out curled up in an armchair. Levi carefully draped a blanket over her. Carl was spread-eagled on the couch, snoring. Mr. Meow sat on the back of the sofa, watching him, apparently confused by the noise he was making.

"Dacian!" I said in a hushed voice when he appeared in the living room. "What are you doing here?" I beckoned him to follow me into the kitchen.

"It's about the storm," he replied, nodding hello to Levi, who was pouring us both a coffee.

The power had held out, but we were prepared with dozens of candles from the shop. I'd done as Levi had requested and removed the magic seal. We'd stood on the staircase at the back of the store and watched as the water squeezed through the gaps, trickling into the shop.

"It's bad," Levi said, handing me a coffee. I wrapped my fingers around it, enjoying the warmth. I'd decided I didn't like being on Earth during storms. It was too cold and wet.

"Yeah, well, it's going to get worse," Dacian said.

"What do you mean?"

"It's no ordinary storm. Well, we don't think it is."

"Explain!" I demanded.

"Ashliel has been keeping an eye on things, you know since y'all were worried about unleashing the white horseman."

"*This is the horseman?*"

"Not unless it's a seahorse!" Dacian shook his head, chuckling. "But no, this is something else. And it's not Mother Nature, either, before you ask."

"If it's not the horseman or Mother Nature, what the hell is it?" Levi was back to growling.

"We think it might be...a dragon."

SIXTEEN

"Dragons are real?" Levi's voice rose so high I could have sworn someone had kicked him in the nuts.

"Most things are real." I shrugged, turning my attention back to Dacian. "A dragon. You're sure?"

"About eighty percent."

"What makes Ash think it's a dragon?"

"For starters, this storm?" Dacian pointed at the window. "It's not showing as a storm. It's not happening."

"I beg to differ," I snorted.

"Exactly," Dacian nodded.

"What?" Levi shook his head in confusion.

"The storm is a disruption in the atmosphere

that occurs when a sleeping dragon wakes," Dacian told us. "At first, we weren't entirely sure, but just before I left, Ash noticed something else."

"What?"

"Movement. Just a twitch, but beneath the earth—way, way, way, beneath the earth—there was a slight movement."

"Fuck!"

If what Dacian had said was true, we were in serious trouble. The dragons had been sleeping for hundreds of years, and as they awoke, Earth would experience earthquakes. Big, destructive, devastating earthquakes. Because the truth was, earthquakes were not the tectonic plates moving, as scientists believed. They were dragons moving—rolling over, maybe yawning—before going back to sleep. But if they were to truly wake up? They'd find their way to the surface, and in the process, destroy whatever was above them.

"Do we know how many dragons?"

"Ashliel is trying to find out. She's also trying to figure out where they are and where they're likely to break through."

"Stop! Just fucking stop for one second!" Levi's voice was no longer high. Now it was low, dangerously low. "Someone explain to me what the fuck is going on! Dragons? We're talking about fire-breathing motherfucking dragons now?"

"It's okay." I tried to soothe him, but he jerked away from me.

"Are you fucking serious? It's not okay! Dragons!" He shook his head. "Un-fucking-believable." Judging by all the cursing, I figured Levi was reaching his limit, and I couldn't blame him. It had been one thing after another since we first met.

"Dragons are real," I told him. "And they were here, along with the dinosaurs, when this dimension was created. The dragons are different from any other creature in that they stay awake for hundreds of years. Then they sleep for hundreds of years, in caves deep beneath the surface, where they won't be discovered or disturbed."

"And now they're waking up?"

"It seems so."

"And you don't see the coincidence in this?"

"What do you mean, coincidence?" Dacian interrupted.

"The seal on the hidden door to the chamber where her father was trapped? That seal was the shape of a dragon."

He was right. It had been a dragon within a circle. Did we do this? By breaking the seal, we hadn't released the white horseman. We'd woken the dragons.

"Lucy?" Levi turned to me, waiting for my answer, most likely expecting a plan of action for dealing with this. I didn't have one. How were we supposed to put a dragon back to sleep?

"We're going to have to go back to Hell," I said, pacing the kitchen floor, thinking, trying to come up with a plan. I didn't remember much about the dragons. I'd have to research them.

"No can do," Dacian said. "Ashliel warned me that I might not be able to get through due to the static in the dimension the dragons are inciting. She said it will settle when they're either fully awake or sleeping again, but we can't cross dimensions while they're in flux. Not safely."

"Fan-bloody-tastic." Levi downed his coffee, slamming his cup a little too hard onto the kitchen bench. I opened my mouth, but before I could get a word out, he rounded on me, finger in my face. "Do not say you're sorry! This isn't your fault, so stop apologizing for someone else's wrong-doing!"

"But if we hadn't broken the seal..."

"Whoever trapped your dad set the seal. This plan has been a long time in the making. Eventually, *someone* would have set the wheels in motion, whether you or another person. It doesn't mean you're to blame. The fault is with whoever set the seals up in the first place. Don't accept blame that isn't due to you."

"He has a point," Dacian agreed. "It can't be a coincidence that you broke a seal with a dragon symbol, and then the dragons started to wake up. We don't know how to put them back to sleep or if it's even possible, so our next best option is to find out who set a trap for your dad and rigged the seal. Did they put the dragons to sleep in the first place? Or did they wait until the dragons slept of their own volition, then lay the trap for your dad?"

My head was spinning with possibilities, and a spark of anger flared to life. How I missed my quiet days in Hell, where my most pressing problems were sinners who wouldn't break or sinners who constantly broke and begged me to ease up on their punishment, with no genuine remorse in their hearts. It was easy. Simple. But this? The dragons who'd been slumbering beneath the earth for eons were starting to stir. How was I supposed to deal with that? And now, cut off from Hell, I couldn't research them, couldn't find the information I needed to determine my next steps.

"Don't lose your shit, Lucy." Dacian watched me with narrowed eyes, recognizing the signs of my anger. "We've got enough going on."

"And you." Dacian rounded on Levi. "Calm down. You getting worked up is only working her up, and when Lucifer gets pissed off, especially in this dimension, fire storms tend to roll across the land."

"It might dry up the water?" Levi shrugged, apparently unconcerned.

"It might. But it would definitely toast the humans, and do you think she's going to be happy about that once she's calmed down? Her temper doesn't come out very often, and for a good reason. Let's not prod the beast, okay?"

"The beast?" Another rumble of thunder, but this time it wasn't the storm outside. It was my own.

"Just a figure of speech," Dacian assured me. I kept my gaze on him and sucked in a deep breath. He was right. Now was not the time for a tantrum, no matter how much I needed it. I wanted to wail and scream and punch something. Hard.

"Why not use some of that energy and go searching for the dragon?" Dacian suggested. "Or dragons. Since Shadow Falls is experiencing this weather event, I think it's safe to assume that more than one dragon is under us."

"You could be right. There are caverns and tunnels beneath Shadow Falls, and I wondered why the first time I discovered them."

"You think it's for the dragon?"

"Dragon worshippers, at the very least. They exist." The more I thought about it, the more it made sense. Shadow Falls was a magnet for the paranormal. The veil here was thin between this dimension and the rest. Why wouldn't a dragon choose to slumber beneath its surface?

"I'll come with you."

I shook my head. "No. Levi, you stay here and keep Sophie and Carl safe. Dacian, can you go searching for anyone who's stuck and needs help? This flood came on so quickly. I bet a lot of people have been caught out. You can get to them. Bring them here if you have to."

"Are you sure?" Levi grabbed my wrist and tugged me to him. "I don't like the idea of you out there alone."

"I'm Lucifer, Queen of Hell, remember? My strength has returned, and a dragon isn't going to faze me. As long as I know the people of Shadow

Falls are okay, then I can focus on the task on hand."

"I'm not happy about you going alone."

"You don't have to be," I told him, determination in the set of my jaw. I'd been all over the place emotionally since finding my father, but this gave me something concrete to focus on. Another problem that needed solving. As much as I was pissed off about the circumstances, it also had my adrenaline spiking, and I was keen to bust my way through the earth searching for a dragon.

"Be safe." Levi relented, pressing a kiss against my mouth. He pulled away before it could deepen into anything further. "I'll get some food going. Can't believe the power has held out this long. Might as well make the most of it."

"I'll be back soon," I promised.

Leaving his apartment, Dacian behind me, I made my way to the roof, where the wind viciously whipped at us, and the rain was blinding. Turning to Dacian, I shouted, "Fly them back here. Don't worry about them seeing your true form. I'll wipe their memories later."

"Got it. What if there are too many and they don't fit in the apartment?"

"Take them somewhere else, to high ground. The highest building in town. I'll find you."

Nodding, he spread his wings and took off into the night. A second later, I followed suit, heading toward the town center, where the yellow police tape still surrounded the crater that led to the caverns below. With a grim smile, I plunged down into the abyss. Time to go dragon hunting.

SEVENTEEN

I searched the existing tunnels, caverns, and caves and found nothing. But of course, this wasn't deep enough. A dragon would have been discovered this close to the surface. Blasting through the rock, I kept going down, further and further, until I broke into a cave. Using magic to light my way, I slowly made my way further into the massive cavern. If there was a dragon in here, the last thing I wanted to do was startle it.

The cave broke off into tunnels, not dissimilar to those above, and I wondered if they'd been built to mimic these ones. Did the dragon worshippers know about this? Reaching a dead end, I turned on my heel to backtrack when a breeze hit the back of my neck. Spinning back around, I peered at the rock wall before me. And waited. Eventually, I found what I was looking for. An opening appeared, and another gust of wind stirred my hair before it closed again.

"Okay," I said, "I see you. Very clever, I truly thought you were a rock."

An eyelid slowly opened, revealing a golden eyeball. The nostril flared, and the mouth opened in a grin. What I'd thought was a rock wall was actually the hide of a dragon, and he'd been playing with me.

"Why are you here?" he asked, his voice deep and slow.

"I think I may have awakened you. I came to find out if it truly is time for you to wake, or...?"

The dragon sighed, and the wet, steamy gust blew my hair blew back from my face. I stepped sideways to avoid his breaths.

"How would you awaken me?" he asked, turning his massive head toward me.

I quickly moved further back toward the main cave. "Shall we talk out here, where it's not so...cozy?"

"Are you scared I'll burn you, human?"

"Not at all. For one, I'm not human. I'm Lucifer,

an Arch Angel. And two, I run Hell. Fire is my game. You can't burn me."

"What is Hell?" he asked, lumbering toward me. He was so big that my head only reached his knee, and I couldn't help it. I felt just a little intimidated. A first for me.

"It's another dimension. Kind of like Heaven, only it's for the bad guys. You haven't heard of it?"

He shook his head, his tail striking the tunnel wall. Rocks fell. I hurried along the tunnel before he caved it in on us both. When I set foot in the cave, I flew into the middle and waited, watching as the dragon emerged, stretching his wings and neck once he cleared the confines of the tunnel.

"Why haven't you heard of Hell?" I asked once he'd reached me. "There were dragons on Earth when man arrived. God made Hell not long after he created man. You should know about it."

The dragon dropped his head, his breath blowing out onto the ground and sending up clouds of dust.

"I'm...lost." His voice was sorrowful, as were his beautiful golden eyes. Now that we were out in the cave, I could see his scales were a deep emerald and gold color. He was stunning.

"What do you mean?"

"I'm cut off from my family, from the other dragons. Someone tricked me, placed a spell on me."

"Tell me," I encouraged. This could be the link I was looking for.

"I'd laid my first egg and was guarding it in my nest when she came. She said she needed my help. She told me I didn't have to do much and that in return, she would ensure my egg—my baby—would always be watched over and live a long and healthy life." I filed away the fact that what I'd thought was a male dragon was actually a female and made a mental note to not insult her by accidentally referring to her as a male. That wouldn't go down well at all.

"What was her name? What did she look like?"

"She looks a lot like you. Her name is Lilith. And she took my baby." The last words were said with a roar, and flames flew from the dragon's mouth.

"I'm so sorry." I was doing what Levi hated—apologizing for someone else's actions—but someone had stolen this dragon's baby. How could my mother be so cruel?

"You look like her. You know her." The dragon rounded on me, fury in her eyes, and I raised my hands, spread my wings, and rose until we were eye level.

"She's my mother, and I swear, this is the first I knew of any of this."

"Where is my baby? Did it hatch?"

"I honestly don't know. You've been asleep way too long. You should have had several cycles by now, yet this is your first sleep, yes?"

"Yes. My baby, my egg, was the first."

Holy shit. Mother had stolen the very first dragon egg ever laid. Why? And why this elaborate trap? Why seal Father in a hidden tomb in Hell and create the seal that would awaken the dragon whose egg she'd stolen? None of it made any sense.

"I know dragons can communicate telepathically. Are any others awake?"

She blinked slowly, then shook her head. "Enough of this," she said, swishing her tail in agitation. "I must find my baby."

"Wait! Wait!" I cried. "Earth has changed *a lot* since you were last awake. There are millions of people and not much forest."

"So?" A puff of steam rolled over me, heating my skin and leaving it damp and slimy.

"You'll not only kill a lot of them when you rise through the earth, but I'm afraid—" I paused, thinking how to word what I needed to say. "—I'm afraid they'll hurt you or try to kill you. Humans have come a long way. They have weapons now. Powerful weapons that could hurt you. And dragons haven't been seen on Earth for over three hundred years."

"I'm not afraid of humans." Another swish of her tail and another hot breath of steam.

"You should be. Believe me. Look, your baby isn't on the surface. I'd know it if we had a dragon roaming around. And neither is Lilith. But I'm going to find her, and I'll do my best to find your baby, too." I didn't want to think that this poor dragon's baby was dead. That would be too awful to consider, but my mother had stolen the egg for a reason. I had to find out why.

"How can I trust that you're not tricking me, like Lilith?"

"Because I'm not going to put you to sleep. I'm going to ask you to wait here. I'm going to get answers for you, find the truth, and then I'm going to come back. I promise. I'm an Arch Angel, and my word is my bond."

"Child of God?"

I nodded. "Child of God."

A few seconds passed. I didn't think she was going to believe me, but finally, she sank down onto her haunches, tucked her tail around her body, and lowered her head onto her front legs.

"Very well. I will wait one day, and then I will search for my baby. And Lilith."

"How about two days?" I hedged, trying to buy more time. I didn't know where Lilith was or how I'd go about finding her. And if I was stuck on Earth, unable to travel between dimensions, I was screwed.

"One day." For the briefest of moments, her eyes flashed red, and I knew I'd pushed as far as I could with her. She was a mama dragon who was missing her child. My heart hurt for her, for what my mother had done. How could she?

"I'll be back. I promise."

She didn't answer, just closed her eyes and blew out another breath.

I left, flying back the way I'd come, up through the layers of the earth, until I was back in the town square. It was still dark, but the storm had stopped. There was no wind or rain, and while the ground was saturated and limbs had fallen from trees, it was over.

"Are the dragons here?" Levi asked as soon as I stepped through the door of his apartment.

I shook my head. "No. From what I could work

out, it's just one dragon. A dragon that Lilith spelled and then stole her egg."

"What? Why?"

"I don't know. But the dragon has given me one day to find out before she comes up to look for her baby. And Lilith."

"Do you know where her baby is?"

"I've got no clue. I had no idea about any of this. It was put into action eons ago. But it's all connected, and it all seems to be coming back to my mother. She spelled a dragon and stole its egg—not just any egg, but the first dragon egg ever laid on Earth—then somehow trapped my dad in a hidden tomb in Hell, with a spell that, when broken, would wake the dragon. Why? I have absolutely no idea."

Levi pulled me into a tight embrace. "We need to find Lilith."

"We do," I agreed, wrapping my arms around his waist and resting my head on his chest. This had turned into such a mess. Instead of getting answers, I was only getting more questions.

"Where do you think we should start?" he asked.

"Heaven. Dad said her name and bolted. He knows something about all of this. It had to have been her who trapped him. He might not know where she is, but he knows something, and I'm not leaving without answers."

EIGHTEEN

Now that the dragon was awake and the storm was over, we could travel between dimensions again. I'd found Dacian and instructed him to remain on Earth to assist the humans in recovering from the storm damage. Ordinarily, I wouldn't have interfered, but this wasn't any old storm. Ultimately, this was my mother's fault, and it wasn't fair that humans had to suffer because of it.

Levi had insisted on coming with me. He sensed just how much this latest blow had hurt. My mother, whom I'd always forgiven for abandoning me as a child, had done something worse. Something...evil. That was hard to stomach. In fact, the knot of angst in my belly right now was turning and roiling, and I wanted to vomit. Everything I thought to be true *wasn't*. My whole world was changing so fast, and I couldn't keep up.

"You okay?" Levi laced his fingers with mine as we landed at the top of the stairway to Heaven and walked through the Pearly Gates. Dacian had been right. Heaven was healed, and all was as it should be. The gates were pristine and standing wide open, allowing souls entry. The angel at the gate nodded at us in greeting.

"I'm—" I didn't know what to say. I was shell-shocked. I couldn't believe my mother was behind such horrible deeds. Add to that the recent discovery that my father hadn't been busy but trapped in a tomb for thousands of years without my knowledge, and I felt lower than a snake's belly. What sort of daughter was I?

"I don't think I've ever seen you so quiet." Levi nudged me with his shoulder, and I tried to smile, but it faltered and failed. So much was going on in my head that I just couldn't voice.

"Thank you for being here with me," I said instead. His support meant the world. I needed him —his strength, his love. He kept me going when I wanted to curl into a ball and cry. I prided myself on living a life of discipline and order, but I was now in a world of chaos, doubt, and confusion. And I didn't like it, not one bit.

A silver hovercar glided up and stopped next to us, waiting. Blowing out a breath, I slid into the back seat, Levi right behind me. "Angel Towers," I instructed the driverless vehicle, then leaned back as we smoothly pulled away, gazing at Heaven's pristine streets.

"It looks good here," Levi said, gazing out the window.

"Yeah, different from last time, huh? *This* is Heaven." The streets were busy again, flowers were blooming, and people were smiling. All was as it should be, yet I still had that heavy feeling in the pit of my stomach. I just couldn't shake it. I was waiting for the other shoe to drop.

The closer we got to Angel Towers, the more the pit in my stomach grew, and from it came a tiny spark of anger at both my parents. At my dad for draining me so severely and then leaving without an explanation. As for my mom, what she'd been up to was anyone's guess, but everything came back to the two of them, and my anger about getting dragged into their marital squabble inched up a notch or three.

"You're angry." Levi slid his palm over my knee, squeezing.

"I'm furious," I agreed, my calm voice masking my inner turmoil. I'd gone from a weepy emotional mess to an anger-filled angel within seconds, and somewhere in the back of my mind, I questioned my mood swings. But I shrugged it off almost as soon as the thought occurred. Of course, I was all over the place. My parents were up to something and dragging everyone else into their stupid games.

A rumble of thunder vibrated through the vehicle, and Levi squeezed my knee again, which resulted in a tiny electrical charge shooting across his hand.

"Ouch!" He snatched his hand away and frowned at me, then laughed. "Don't say sorry, for fuck's sake! That was unexpected, but I can't say I didn't like it." He winked and placed his hand back on my leg, only this time higher up. Cheeky bastard. I leaned over and kissed his cheek—not the kiss he was looking for because we didn't have time for anything else. We'd arrived at Angel Towers.

"We're here." It was redundant and entirely obvious, but I voiced the words nonetheless. My anger still bubbled beneath the surface, diluted a fraction by Levi's flirting.

"Come on then." Climbing out of the car, Levi held his hand out, waiting for me to place mine in it. Helping me out of the vehicle, he slung an arm around my shoulders, and together we looked up at Angel Towers. I hadn't noticed how dull it was on my last visit, but it was startlingly obvious now due to the holy glow emanating from the massive structure. It had been absent the last time we were here.

"I take it that means God is in?" Levi asked.

"It always did have a glow. I'd forgotten," I admitted.

Crossing the foyer, I ignored the angels who turned and stared at us and the whispering that ensued. The last time I'd visited, the lobby had been deserted, but now that God had returned, his mere presence attracted the angels like moths to a flame.

We remained silent on the ride up. I was concentrating on keeping a lid on my anger. I'd fought long and hard to stay professional where my brothers were concerned, and to have a temper tantrum in front of them was not high on my agenda. I couldn't wait to see Dad, get all the details from him, and find out once and for all what the hell was going on. I also wanted to know whether my brothers had known all along. If they had, I was going to kick their asses from here to Hell; consequences be damned. The elevator shook a little, and Levi chuckled.

"You're going to rip him a new one, aren't you?" he asked conversationally.

"I'm going to try not to. But...I'm pissed off." I had no intention of pretending I wasn't angry and hurt.

The elevator stopped, and the doors slid open, revealing the boardroom. The last time I'd been here, Gabriel was sitting at the head of the table. Now it was Dad. I stopped, my eyes taking him in. He hadn't aged a day. Chestnut brown hair shone under the lights, his blue eyes twinkled, and the dimple in his cheek appeared as a welcoming smile lit up his face.

"Lucifer! I'm so pleased you came." He stood, and I noticed the robes he used to wear were gone. Now he was dressed in a snappy charcoal suit. The long hair that he'd always worn in a bun was now stylishly cut, and he was clean-shaven. So different, and yet the same.

"Dad," I responded, stopping at the opposite end of the massive boardroom table. Levi stood just to the left of me.

"And Levi." Dad smiled at him. "I have to thank

you for looking after my daughter." He headed toward us, arm outstretched, looking to shake Levi's hand. I stepped in between them, blocking him.

"About that." My voice was cold. "About how you almost killed me, stole all my magic, and then left me for dead." A loud clap of thunder shook the room, and Dad stopped, a frown drawing his eyebrows together.

"Lucifer, no. That's not how it was." He was genuinely surprised, and it was all I could do not to raise my hand and shoot a fireball at him. How dare he? How dare he suck me dry, leave me, and then be surprised that I'd feel this way?

"Sweetheart." He reached out, but I backed away, bumping into Levi, who settled his hands on my shoulders, his presence comforting. "I left in a hurry because I had to stop your mother."

I laughed. "She was long gone, and you knew it. You had to have known you were trapped in there for a long time."

"I lost track of time, but from the wasting of my body, I knew hundreds, if not thousands, of years had passed. But I'm immortal. I cannot die. I just had to wait it out. And you found me. Saved me."

"And you couldn't hang around long enough to say thank you?"

He cocked his head, then looked down at his shoes before meeting my eyes, the same shade of blue as his own.

"You're right. I apologize. I now understand how it must have seemed to you—that I took your magic to heal myself and then returned to Heaven without you."

"I didn't want you to bring me with you, Dad! I wanted you to stay. I wanted you to care enough to make sure I was okay. And I wanted an explanation as to what the hell was going on. Who trapped you in there and why?"

"It was your mother," he responded with absolute certainty. "Sit," he ordered, spinning on his heel to return to his seat at the head of the table. Not wanting to shout over the length of the table, I chose a seat in the middle. Levi sat next to me, once more resting his hand on my knee. I covered it with my own, squeezing it back. I felt calm. In control. The anger was still there and could quickly erupt, but for now, I was in control.

"You're certain it was mother?" I asked.

"Yes."

"Did you see her?"

"She sent me a message when I was creating Hell to meet her there. She wanted to talk."

"What about?"

He shrugged. "I don't know. I hadn't seen nor heard from her since she left me." Did I detect a hint of sadness in his voice? A touch of pain?

"Us," I corrected automatically. She hadn't just left him. She'd left us, her children.

"Us," he agreed.

"Then what happened? She sent you a message, and you agreed to meet her?"

"Yes. In the chamber. Hell was nearly finished. But I didn't want you to see her and get your hopes up, so the chamber was the best place. I think she was counting on that."

"Oh?"

"I was waiting for her, only she didn't show up on time. That wasn't unusual for Lilith. She was always late for everything. Then I heard her call my name. She was in this antechamber, just off the main room. I walked in, and the door slammed shut. I heard her voice but couldn't make out the words. I know now it was a spell, sealing the door. Sealing the room. I couldn't get out. My magic wouldn't work. I couldn't blast through the walls, floor, or ceiling. I kept a light burning for as long as I could so I wasn't in darkness, but eventually...well, I needed what was left to keep myself alive."

We were silent, digesting his words.

"Why? Why did she do that?" I finally asked.

"I don't know!" He slammed a hand down on the table, making me jump. "Sorry." His apology was immediate and sincere. I'd rarely witnessed my father's anger, but I could see it in him now as he relived what she'd done to him. "I don't know why she did it, and after so many years apart. I would understand it better if it had happened right after we split, but years later?"

"Do you know about the dragons?" I asked.

"What about them?"

"There's one beneath Shadow Falls that was awakened when we broke the seal to get you out. It told me that Lilith stole its egg. Its baby."

He blew out a breath, running a hand through his newly-styled hair. On an ordinary man, the strands would have stuck up all over the place, but this was God, and each strand fell back into place, unruffled.

"I had a plan for the dragons that I assumed your brothers would see through. There should be no dragons on Earth."

"Well, there are," I pointed out. "One, at least. And what do you mean, no dragons? Did you plan to make them extinct?"

"I never make my creations extinct, Lucifer, you know that."

"Yeah, yeah, you move them off to other dimensions, other worlds, when you think it's getting too dangerous for them on Earth. Was that your plan for the dragons?"

He nodded. "I made them for your mother to remind her of her home. When she left, I decided the dragons could go with her."

"Then why would she trick a dragon, spell it, and steal its egg when they were hers anyway? And why connect all of that to the seal on the room she imprisoned you in?"

"They are questions I cannot answer. Only Lilith can answer them," Dad said.

"And where is she?" I asked.

"I assume she's with her family in the Qanyl dimension. I have sent a message requesting an audience. She—they—have yet to respond."

"Why not just go there and demand to see her?"

"That would start a war. A war among the gods is not wise."

Silence fell again. We were all lost in our own thoughts. Then I asked, "Where are Gabriel and Michael?" I had yet to see my brothers, and I'd been expecting them to be here by God's side.

"They are…elsewhere," Dad said, not meeting my eyes.

"Where exactly?"

We stared at each other, then I burst out, "You had better not have sent them to Hell! I do not want their sorry asses in my home. Let them repent their sins somewhere else."

"They have done wrong. They have lied, manipulated, and hurt others, all for their own gain."

"Yes, I know, but come on. Hell? Really? Since when was Hell designed to punish angels?" And why hadn't Ashliel alerted me to the fact that my brothers had turned up?

"Ashliel received direct instructions not to discuss this matter with you," Dad said.

"Stop reading my mind." My anger rumbled again, and a spark of red electricity shot from my fingers. "Hell is my dimension. I've run it exactly as you instructed. I've done a good job. No, I've done a brilliant job. For you to go behind my back and instruct *my* people not to tell me things, that is unacceptable." Pushing my chair back, I rose, body vibrating. How dare he? How fucking dare he!

"You have gotten too used to my absence, Lucifer!" His words were sharp, but he didn't stand.

Instead, he steepled his fingers in front of him and stared at me. His tactics might have worked once, but not any longer. I was my own woman now, and while God's word was law here, my word was law in my dimension.

"You overstep," I retorted. "You may have created Hell, but I've made it into what it is today. I'm in charge. Not you." It was a challenge, one he couldn't ignore. A part of me wanted to back down and apologize, but another part was dancing and yahooing and saying, *you go, girl*!

We eyeballed each other for several long, silent seconds. Levi's hand had frozen in a death grip on my knee, one that would likely leave bruises, but I didn't move to dislodge it. I didn't move at all. I would not back down. I would stand up for what was mine. Fight for what was mine. And Hell was mine.

"Very well." Breaking eye contact, he looked to Levi, then back at me. What had just happened? I'd won an argument with God? "You are right. You've done a wonderful job with Hell. You took it upon yourself to help on Earth when the soul stealer broke through, and you were instrumental in finding me and breaking the spell that kept me imprisoned. All the while, your brothers were here, plotting and scheming, letting Heaven and Earth suffer."

"And what is their punishment exactly? Because don't for one second think you can send them to *my* dimension and give them cushy jobs in Hell HQ."

"Their punishment is for you to decide. You do run Hell, after all." He grinned, feeling pleased with himself.

My frown deepened. "Oh, no. You're taking the easy way out, and that's not fair. They're not human. They're your problem, and you're palming them off on to me. No way. You need to deal with them."

"Oh really?" His laugh was incredulous.

"Dad! They are your sons. My brothers. If they stay in Hell, it will be in the fiery pit because I've had it up to here—" I indicated with a hand across my throat. "—with those assholes. Is that what you really want? Them screaming in agony while I burn the skin from their bones every day?" I turned to Levi. "I can't believe I'm trying to talk my dad out of letting me do that. I mean, after all their bullshit, maybe I should keep them with me for a bit."

"Is that truly what you'd do?" Dad asked.

"How else would you punish an angel in Hell?

Nothing else would be effective. All or nothing for my brothers."

"Very well. I shall retrieve them."

"Why not send them to Earth without their angelic powers? Make them live as the humans they so despise?" Levi suggested.

"That is brilliant!" I smiled, then laughed. "They'd hate it! It's perfect."

"I do agree it does have a certain sense of justice to it," God said. "It is done."

"What? Already?" Levi asked in surprise. "I didn't see your hand move or anything."

"I'm God. My wish is my command." His chest puffed out ever so slightly, and I sighed. Men and their egos.

"Back to the topic of Mom. Because we still have a dragon problem on Earth. I promised the dragon I'd be back in one day with her egg; otherwise, she's going to burst through and create all sorts of havoc in Shadow Falls. And ultimately get herself killed because that's what the humans will do when faced with a real, live dragon."

"We may have a bigger problem," Dad replied.

My stomach dropped to my toes. Just when things were getting sorted out, what next? "What?" I asked.

"She planned all this for a reason. There's more coming. Something big."

"But...this was hundreds of years ago. Maybe she's cooled off? Changed her mind?"

"Doubtful. We still don't know why she did it. And you can be certain that she would have been alerted that you broke the spell, I'm free, and the dragon is awake."

He was right. We were screwed.

NINETEEN

"So, what do we do?" I started pacing, my mind unable to focus.

"We wait," Dad responded, his calmness an irritation that had my eyes flaring flames.

"We cannot afford to wait, Dad. Haven't you been listening? A dragon is about to bring its wrath onto the citizens of Shadow Falls. The *innocent* citizens of Shadow Falls. And I've already told you what will happen next—we don't need Levi's psychic abilities for that. The army will respond with deadly force and blow that poor dragon off the face of the planet. And then study the body parts left behind. Is that how you want this to go down? Is that what you want people to remember, to think of when they learn that God has returned?"

"Your caring nature is one of the reasons I chose you to run Hell. It pleases me that you are still the strong-minded, strong-willed, kind angel I remember." He beamed at me, but I wanted to smack him.

"Dad! Do something!"

He chuckled, then sighed, shaking his head. "Very well. I have retrieved the dragon, and she is being cared for. Happy?"

"No. I'm far from happy." I pouted. "I still need to find Mom and either get the egg back or find the baby."

"Um, Lucy?" Levi interrupted. "That egg would have hatched a long time ago if it was fertile. And that baby? If all this happened hundreds of years ago, well, that baby would be either full-grown or dead by now."

Fuck, he was right. "Where are all the dragons, Dad? Did you send them on to Mom? Keep them here? Leave them on Earth?" If Mom already had the dragons, why did she need another one? Would she want the one she'd left behind on Earth, or didn't she care? She'd walked away from her own children easily enough. One dragon wasn't likely to cause her any heartache.

"When she left, I attempted to contact her many times, initially to try to make amends and repair our marriage." I could hear the guilt in his voice. He blamed himself for the marriage breakdown and Mom leaving. "But all communication was cut off. I assumed she returned to the Qanyl dimension, to her family, but they blocked me. I sent a gift, but it was destroyed. I dared not send the dragons in case they would be destroyed, too."

"What did you do with them, then?"

"Created a pocket dimension for them. An annex to Heaven, if you like, where there are no humans to hunt them."

"And they're still there?"

"Yes. She can have them. They're hers. And I've never stopped trying to reach out to her, only it's been a while because, you know, she trapped me in Hell."

We were interrupted by the elevator arriving. I was surprised Father would allow anyone to disturb him, for I knew the elevator would not deliver anyone to this floor without his permission. I smiled when Dacian stepped out.

"Welcome, Dacian." Dad's voice echoed, and I cringed.

"Dad, cut it out. You don't need to put on the full God voice for anyone. This is Dacian, our friend."

Dad had the grace to look sheepish. Dacian did a slight, awkward bow.

"Relax," I chided. "It's just my dad."

"Yes, but I'm a Seraph angel. It's sort of automatic."

"Dad, please tell him to relax. Dacian is not only a dear friend, but I consider him to be a brother to me. More than my own brothers have ever been."

"Brother? Last I knew, you two were romantically involved." Casting a quick glance at Levi, he muttered, "Sorry, Levi."

"We were. And it ended. And now we're friends." I resumed my seat next to Levi and slid my hand into his, reassuring him. He had no reason to be jealous of Dacian, and I hoped we were past all that. He squeezed my hand in response.

"How did it go on Earth?" I asked, changing the subject. "All good?"

"Yes, although I will need you to go and do your mind wipe thing. There was no avoiding being seen during the storm, considering I was flying humans to safety."

"Urgh, I'd forgotten. I should go now before they jump on social media and plaster it all over the place."

"It is done," Dad said.

"Already? You don't have to be face to face with them?" I was surprised.

"They are my creations. I can control them any way I choose. Mostly I allow them free will. But, on occasions like this, when heavenly intervention is required…" His words faded, and he shrugged.

"Where are Gabriel and Michael?" Dacian asked. "I should check in before I get dragged to HR again." He clapped a hand over his mouth and looked from me to God and back again as if just realizing what he'd said.

"He knows everything," I assured Dacian, patting the chair to my left. "Come sit. I assume you wanted Dacian here for a reason?" I directed my words at Dad.

"Michael and Gabriel are no longer in Heaven, nor do they hold positions of power at Angel Towers," Dad told him. "Instead, I want to talk to you about a promotion."

"Oh?" Dacian squeaked, then, adjusting his collar, said in a lower tone, "Oh?"

Dad smiled. "I would like to offer you the

position of Vice President of Defense. You've practically been doing the job anyway, and there is no one more worthy than you. You will be directly responsible for Heaven's armies and defenses. You'll also receive the appropriate remuneration. Interested?"

"I would be honored." Dacian bowed his head again, and I bit back a snort. He deserved this. He'd earned it.

"What about the Vice President of Invention?" I asked.

"I will recruit for that position, as well as your old role, Lucifer—Vice President of Galactic Expansion. It's time for some new blood and direction."

"That's what you used to do, Lucy?" Levi asked. "Vice President of Galactic Expansion?"

"Yup. I looked after housing, development, and population control in Heaven, and I supervised planetary exploration."

"Wow, that's...huge."

I grinned. "Not as huge as being the CEO of Hell."

"Ashliel would make an admirable Vice President of Galactic Expansion," Dad commented.

I shot him a look. "Oh, no. No poaching my staff.

Plus, Ashliel loves it in Hell. I doubt she'd want to return here."

"Have you asked her?"

"Dad, don't push me on this. Post your vacancies. If she wants to apply, she can, but you cannot approach her and offer her the position. Understood?"

"You've gotten pushy," he grumbled, but the smile turning up his lips told me he wasn't angry.

We lapsed into silence, each lost in our own thoughts until Dacian turned to me and said, "Your energy is still off."

"What?" I was surprised. I felt normal, despite my mood being all over the place, but then that wasn't surprising, given all that had happened recently.

"Haven't you noticed it, Levi?" Dacian asked him.

Levi shrugged. Wait? Had he noticed and not said anything? Why? "Levi?"

"It isn't Levi you should be asking, my child. It is your father."

We all gasped, heads spinning toward the female voice that came from behind us. I hadn't heard the elevator arrive.

"Lilith!" Dad stood up so fast his chair toppled

over. My eyes drank in the raven-haired woman before us.

Mother.

TWENTY

"Hello, Lucifer, my darling." She strolled in, tall and elegant and so, so beautiful. I was lost for words. Dacian lunged to his feet and took up a protective stance in front of Dad.

"It's okay, Dacian." Dad rested his hand on Dacian's shoulder. "Stand down."

Dacian didn't move a muscle, ignoring Dad's instructions. Lilith chuckled.

"Insubordinate little angel." She winked at Dacian. "I like him."

"Lilith." The words came out choked, and Dad cleared his throat.

I glanced at him to see his eyes glassy, full of tears. He still loved her. After everything that had happened, he still loved her. I turned to look at her, this stunning woman who had given birth to me. While technically I knew she was my mother, I didn't feel that connection with her. She was a vaguely familiar stranger.

"No hug for your mommy, Lucifer?" She opened her arms wide, waiting for me to rush into them. I stayed seated, turning my head to gaze instead at the tabletop.

"Well," she puffed, "that's disappointing. But not entirely surprising." I felt her pass behind us, her hands trailing over the back of our chairs. Levi was ramrod straight next to me, barely breathing. I had so many questions, yet I couldn't voice a single one.

"And Elohim, my love." The purr of her voice had a hard edge beneath it, and I winced. She was the only one who called Dad by his given name. It felt strange to hear it again. "Have you missed me?"

She had almost reached Dacian, and I suddenly felt afraid for him. Lilith was powerful. I hadn't realized it before—had no clue, since I barely remembered her—but like me, she was the daughter of gods. She wasn't without strength.

I pushed myself to my feet, and she spun, a hand catching my chin as she examined my face. She moved in close, and I could feel her breath against my face. I bit back the urge to cringe. This wasn't the reunion I'd daydreamed about as a child.

"Release her, Lilith." Dad found his voice, his tone demanding once more.

"She grew into a beauty." Lilith smiled, dropping her hand and turning her attention back to my father. "Where are my sons?"

He ignored her question. "Why are you here?"

"You knew I would come," she chided him, tutting as she about-faced and slowly, deliberately walked the length of the table until she was standing opposite my father, the length of the table between them.

Without word or warning, she threw a fireball at him. He deflected easily before any of us could react.

"Really, Lilith? Stop with the parlor games." He shook his head as if deeply disappointed in her. Which I supposed he was. Levi and I eyed her warily.

"Stop? Oh, my darling, the fun is just beginning! You took longer than I expected to get out of Hell." She shrugged, her red lips curled up in a smirk. "But now that you are, well, let's just say there's more to come."

"Why?"

"You have to ask me that?" Her anger rolled

through the room, and it felt familiar to me. I was my mother's daughter, after all. No wonder I was so suited to running Hell. Fire was in my blood. "You forced me into this, Eli. I left my family for you. I turned my back on my own heritage for you. And what did I get in return? I was ignored and turned away, time after time when I begged for your love. You were too busy. You always had one more thing to do. Once I'd delivered the children you so desperately wanted, I was nothing to you. Nothing. And I couldn't go home. I was banished for choosing you over them. You left me with nothing. And now that is what I shall leave you with."

"Lilith, I'm sorry. So sorry. More sorry than you'll ever know, ever believe. But I loved you. I truly did. Still do."

"You love the idea of having a dutiful wife," she spat, the air thick with tension. Thunder rolled outside, so familiar to my own angry rumblings that I shivered. Seeing her after all this time was so surreal, yet here she was, bristling with hurt and rage.

"No. I tried to contact you. Over and over again, I tried. But your family blocked me and destroyed any gifts I sent."

"But you never came in person, did you? Never

cared enough to come yourself. Instead, you sent messages, a token gift or two."

"I couldn't get away. I was—" He stopped himself, realizing what he'd been about to say. He'd been too busy creating Hell. His marriage had fallen apart, and he'd made Hell his priority. Not his wife. Ouch. No wonder she was pissed.

Her chin tilted in apparent triumph. "You were saying?"

"What can I do to fix this?" he whispered, the agony apparent in his voice. He truly did love her. A love so great that hundreds of years apart hadn't dimmed it, yet that love had destroyed her. My mother was so full of rage that I wondered if she even could love anymore. And my heart ached at the thought.

"Fix it?" She laughed. A crack of lightning struck the table, leaving a black scorch mark. "You can't fix it. I will fix it. By destroying you—and all you hold dear."

He sucked in a breath. "You would harm our children?"

Again, she laughed, only this time without the lightning. "See? This is what you do. Why would you think I would harm my own children? The children you kept from me? The children that I gave birth to and love? Oh no, my dear Eli, it is you I will harm. I will turn them against you, make them see that the foolish love they think they have for you is nothing but a lie."

"I do love them, as I love you. With all my heart."

"You can keep saying that until your dying breath, and I will never believe you. Now, where are my sons? I demand to see them!"

"They're not here."

"Summon them," she demanded, waving a perfectly manicured hand through the air.

"I will not." I was surprised he'd defied her.

"Very well. I will start with Lucifer. She will be the most challenging, after all."

"What do you mean?" I demanded.

"You have always been your father's daughter. Gabriel and Michael were mommy's boys, but you? You were daddy's girl. But you need to see him for the flawed man he is, Lucifer."

"We all have flaws. No one is perfect," I replied. I really didn't want to get dragged into this. Still, if their disagreement was going to put Earth in jeopardy, then I'd do my best to help them resolve their differences. Only right now, Mom wasn't looking like she wanted to mend fences. She wanted to burn them down.

"You don't know, do you?" She tapped a finger against her ruby lips, eyes running from the top of my head to the tips of my toes and back again.

"Know what?"

"Has anyone else noticed it?" Ignoring me, she looked at Levi, then Dacian. Dacian shook his head, but Levi lifted one shoulder.

"What?" I whispered to him, but he wouldn't look at me. He had his eyes trained on my mother, and his body was so tense it hurt to look at.

Lilith tipped back her head and laughed, long and loud. "This is too easy!" she chuckled.

"What? What is going on? Someone tell me!" I had that horrible feeling in the pit of my stomach.

"Tell her, Levi," my mother commanded him.

He shook his head. "No."

"What? Levi, what is it? What don't I know? And how do *you* know?"

"I see your reasoning," Mom said to him, then turned her attention back to my dad. "How about you? Care to tell your daughter the truth about what you did?"

Silence.

"Dad?" I whispered. This was bad. This was so, so bad. I knew my world was about to change irrevocably, and I was powerless to stop it.

A tear slid silently down my father's cheek, and my own eyes welled in response. What had he done? What was so bad he couldn't tell me? That Levi wouldn't tell me?

"Very well." Mother sighed in mock irritation just as Dad yelled out, "No!" She ignored him. "Lucifer, your father took your child from you," she said calmly, without inflection.

"What? What child? What are you talking about? I don't have a child." Levi shuffled from foot to foot next to me, and Dad dropped his head to his hands on the table, sobbing. What was going on? Dacian looked as confused as I was.

"When he took your magic to heal himself, you were pregnant. He took your child to sustain his own life," Mother said.

I stopped breathing. Moving. I couldn't so much as blink. I'd been pregnant. How had I not known I was pregnant? Then it began, like a movie playing in my mind. The lovemaking in my office, when Levi had bitten me, marked me like I'd marked him. I saw it now, that tiny spark of life he'd planted in my womb. My hand automatically went to my abdomen, but as much as I searched for it, I knew it was gone. She was right. He'd taken my baby.

"Lucy?" Levi slid his arm around my shoulders,

but I shrugged him off, for the biggest betrayal of all was that he'd known. On trembling legs, I stepped away from him.

"Lucy, please." Now he was begging like my father had been begging my mother only minutes earlier. I looked at her now, expecting to see triumph on her face. Instead, I only saw compassion. Who better to understand the loss of a child than a woman who'd lost her own?

"You knew," I whispered to Levi, my voice broken. So broken, it hurt to talk. "How?"

"My connection to you. Our bond. I sensed our baby's arrival. I wanted you to discover it for yourself, so I didn't say anything. Then, when your dad used your magic to heal himself, I knew it was gone. I knew what he'd done, whether it was intentional or not—and Lucy, I'd like to think it was unintentional—I figured, why tell you? You hadn't known you were pregnant. You were only pregnant for a few short hours. Why upset you more than you already were?"

"That's why your energy has been off," Dacian muttered. I looked at him without seeing him. At least he hadn't known. At least he hadn't kept this from me.

"You knew, though, didn't you, Dad? When you

sucked the life out of me, you knew you'd taken my baby's life."

He continued to cry, head down on the table. It was all the answer I needed.

"Lucy." Levi reached out to me, and I stepped away. I was frozen inside, and I knew that when I defrosted, I was going to be in pain, more pain than I'd ever experienced in my life. She'd been right. My mom had been right.

"Come, sweetheart." She held out her arms to me. I walked into them, too numb to cry. She wrapped me in her embrace, and she smelled so familiar. I closed my eyes and clung to her.

"Lucy! Please. Don't do this. I'm sorry," Levi pleaded with me. But I couldn't look at him. I'd been wrong. The ice in me was starting to melt, and in its place came red-hot anger. I pulled away from my mother to look her in the eye.

"You haven't won me," I told her. "You knew this would hurt me beyond anything. You did it purely to hurt Dad. Well, congratulations, you've succeeded. But in destroying him, you've destroyed me."

"You deserved to know, Lucifer," she said defensively.

"Yes. I did. And it should have been by you." I turned to my father, pointing at him. He sat up, his face wet. "That's why you didn't stick around, isn't it? You ran! You ran hard and fast so you wouldn't have to face the truth of what you'd done!"

"I didn't know. I didn't realize I'd taken your child until I felt it—her. But know that she is a part of me now. She is safe."

"Safe? Are you fucking kidding me? She isn't with me, in me, where she is meant to be! And you!" I turned my rage on Levi. "You *knew*. All this time, you knew and didn't say a word. My mood swings. My strange energy pattern. *You knew*." The last was said on a sob, my own tears falling thick and fast. I spun, turning my back on them all.

I felt him behind me, his hand coming down on my shoulder, trying to pull me into his embrace. No! Never again. I threw him away from me, not caring when I heard the table smash where he landed on it.

"Do not touch me. Do not speak to me. I don't want to see you—any of you—ever again." I didn't recognize my own voice. It was as if a stranger were speaking.

I didn't know if this was what my mother had intended when she arrived in Heaven, but as I departed, angry red clouds sending even angrier red bolts of lightning into Heaven, I was beyond caring. I was no longer interested in her story, in her and

Dad's marital strife, or in her quest for so-called vengeance. I didn't care about anything.

I'd been betrayed by everyone I held dear, betrayed in the worst way. And I'd lost my baby, the baby I hadn't known about, and my heart shattered in my chest at that loss. As I flew back to Hell, there was one thing clear in my mind.

Come hell or high water, they would pay.

TWENTY-ONE

Lucy flung me across the room, and I grunted as I smashed through the heavy wooden table. I couldn't blame her. If I were her, I'd fucking kill me. My own heart hurt at the pain I'd seen in her eyes. She'd been shattered. Ripped apart. And here I was, saying trite words like "I'm sorry." Fuck, this was a mess of epic proportions.

Dacian held out a hand to help me up from the remains of the table, and I accepted. His face revealed nothing, and although I knew his loyalties lay with Lucy—and rightly so—I was glad he hadn't taken it upon himself to kick my ass. I got the feeling he was reserving that right for Lucy.

"Well, that didn't go as expected, but the result

was spectacular, wouldn't you say?" Lilith crowed in triumph once Lucy had departed.

No one answered. We all must have been shocked that she didn't seem to care about the pain she'd just brought down on her own daughter.

"You think I don't care about her?" she said as if she'd read our minds. Maybe she had. "That's where you're wrong. I love her as only a mother can. You both lied to her, continuously, to save your own sorry hides. So don't go blaming me for this. If she'd known the truth, it wouldn't have worked, now, would it?"

She spun on her heel and left. I looked from Dacian to God and back again. I had no idea what to say. God was a mess. While he'd stopped sobbing, tears still leaked from his eyes, and I looked away, uncomfortable at his distress. I briefly wondered if I should be angry about what he'd done, but a part of me had always known he hadn't absorbed our child on purpose. Desiccated, he'd drawn on Lucy's magic like a man dying of thirst.

I should have been furious with him, but the newly-developed demon side of me was keeping me level-headed. This wasn't his fault. Could he have handled it better? Shit, yeah, but then again, the same could be said for me. I should have told Lucy right away when I sensed she was carrying our child. I don't know why I hadn't. But for some reason, I'd wanted to let her discover our child on her own. Perhaps I wanted her to surprise me with the news? I didn't really have an answer.

"I'm sorry," God croaked, reaching out a shaking hand to me. I took it and pulled him into my arms, thumping his back in an awkward embrace.

"It was an accident," I told him.

"It was. If I could change it, I would. I'd return the child to you."

"But you can't." I knew this. She was gone—a daughter, he'd said.

He shook his head. "No. I can't."

I stepped away, not comfortable with all the tears and hugging.

"Now what?" Dacian asked, arms akimbo.

"I've got no idea," I admitted. "I've never seen her like that. I guess we'll just have to give her time to cool off?" It went against every cell in my body to not go after her, to not pull her into my arms and let her cry out all her pain. But she'd just finished throwing me through the table. I got the sense my company would not be appreciated right now.

"You don't understand." God sniffed and straightened his shoulders, pulling himself together.

"Understand what?"

"How do I say this?" he murmured, running both of his hands through his hair and pulling.

I sighed. How bad could it be? "Just say it."

"She's done with you," Dacian said instead, taking me by surprise.

I spun to face him. "What do you mean?" Yes, she'd spat at us that she never wanted to see any of us again, but those were just angry words. *Weren't they?*

"Let me put it in more human terms." His voice held a trace of sarcasm, but I let it slide, for my heart had stopped in my chest. I knew what he was about to say, but I prayed that I was wrong. "She just broke up with you. Those last words of hers, about not wanting to see you—us—ever again? That was for keeps. Forever." He was blunt, but I supposed I needed to hear it.

"No." Although I knew Dacian was right, that Lucy was done with me, I wasn't done with her. There was no way in Heaven or Hell I was letting her go.

And if that meant we had a fight on our hands, so be it.

Lucy and Levi's epic tale continues in **The Devil You Know.** Don't miss the thrilling conclusion of their journey.

Grab your copy now and join them in the final chapter of their spellbinding adventure here: www.JaneHinchey.com/HellsAngel

Thank you for reading! If you enjoyed this book, I'd greatly appreciate your review.

You can find a complete list of my books, including series and reading order on my website at:

www.JaneHinchey.com

Join my newsletter here:

www.JaneHinchey.com/subscribe

And finally, join my readers group on Facebook here:

www.JaneHinchey.com/LittleDevils

Thank you so much for taking a chance and reading my book . It's readers like you who make this journey worthwhile and fuel my passion for storytelling. Your support means the world to me, and I can't wait to share more exciting stories with you in the future.

xoxo

Jane

READ MORE BY JANE

Find them all at www.JaneHinchey.com/books

<u>The Ghost Detective Mysteries</u>

#1 Ghost Mortem

#2 Give up the Ghost

#3 The Ghost is Clear

#4 A Ghost of a Chance

#5 Here Ghost Nothing

#6 Who Ghost There?

#7 Wild Ghost Chase

#8 Easy Come, Easy Ghost

#9 Life Ghost On

<u>Witch Way Paranormal Cozy Mystery Series</u>

#1 Witch Way to Magic & Mayhem

#2 Witch Way to Romance & Ruin

#3 Witch Way Down Under

#4 Witch Way to Beauty & the Beach

#5 Witch Way to Death & Destruction

#6 Witch Way to Secrets & Sorcery

The Gravestone Mysteries

#1 Fur the Hex of it

#2 Battle of the Hexes

#3 What the Hex

The Midnight Chronicles

#1 One Minute to Midnight

#2 Two Minutes Past Midnight

#3 Third Strike of Midnight

Clean Scene Inc.

#1 All in Vein

PARANORMAL ROMANCE/URBAN FANTASY

The Awakening Trilogy

Hell's Angel Trilogy

The Enforcer Series (4 books)

Standalones

Returned

Secret Fates

Destiny's Touch

Blood Cursed

Heart of Darkness

ABOUT JANE

Hi there! I'm Jane, crafting tales of paranormal cozy mysteries sprinkled with urban fantasy romance. Between sips of coffee and dodging my mischievous cats, I immerse myself in stories where magic meets everyday life.

Once known as Zahra Stone in the world of steamy urban fantasy, I've now merged those fiery tales under the Jane Hinchey banner. Off the page you'll find me binging on true crime documentaries or sneaking in a power nap. Dive into my stories and join me on an enchanting journey!

Find me here: www.janehinchey.com

facebook.com/janehincheyauthor

instagram.com/janehincheyauthor

amazon.com/Jane-Hinchey/e/B0193449MI

bookbub.com/authors/jane-hinchey

goodreads.com/jane_hinchey